Table of Contents

Preface iv

Chapter I 1

    Living on a Borrowed Time 3

    A Facilitation Fee 12

    The Checkpoint 17

    A Tale of Deceit 21

    A Silent War 25

    A Bitter Pill of Complicity 31

    A Ghost Shell 37

    A Gnawing Sense of Disillusionment 43

    A Toxic Brew of Despair 47

Chapter II 52

    A Life Sucked Out of the Land 54

    A Squeezed Political Space 60

    A Terrorized Village 64

    Vanished Without a Trace 69

    A Sealed Fate 73

    A Darkness of Insecurity 77

    A Voice of Dissent 81

    A Tapestry of Broken Promises 87

    An Opulent Feast 93

Chapter III 97

An Elusive Prosperity	99
Living by Humanitarian Food	104
A Hollow Victory	111
The Whispers of Discontent	116
A Victim of a Broken Nation	121
A Gnawing Stomach	126
A Thousand Lost Dreams	130
A Wasteland of Hunger	135
A Breeding Ground for Chaos	139
The Brewing Storm	143
A Graveyard of Dreams	147
Chapter IV	**152**
A Broken Promise	154
A Whisper on the Wind.	158
A Forgotten Legion	163
The Paradox of Liberation	167
Chapter V	**172**
Blinded by Greed and Power	174
The Curse of the Unknown	178
The Towering Mountain of Debt	186
The Destructive Machine	190
A Prisoner of His Own Conscience	194
The Architect of Despair	199
A Plan Fueled by Greed	206

A Conquer of Greed...212
A Prisoner of his Own Legacy 217
A Conduit for Personal Fortune............................221
The Promise of Wealth 226

Preface

In the heart of Africa, where the cradle of humanity still whispers its ancient tales, lies a nation whose birth was heralded by the world with a hopeful gaze. South Sudan, the world's youngest country, emerged from the shadows of a protracted struggle, carrying the aspirations of its people towards a horizon of self-determination and prosperity. Yet, the journey from the euphoria of independence to the sobering realities of governance has been fraught with challenges that have tested the resilience of its citizens.

'The Stolen Nation' is not merely a book; it is a mirror reflecting the fragmented soul of a country torn between its liberated past and its encumbered present. Through a collection of 44 short stories, this anthology weaves a narrative that is as diverse as it is poignant, grouped into five chapters that dissect the anatomy of a nation's unhealed wounds and unfulfilled promises.

As you turn the pages of Chapter I, you will traverse the network of corruption that has trapped the very institutions meant to be the pillars of a thriving society. You will witness the erosion of trust and the squandering of hope as the guardians of the state morph into its exploiters, leaving the populace in a state of deprivation and disillusionment.

Chapter II unveils the stark landscape of neglect, where environmental degradation and insecurity bleed into the fabric of daily life, staining it with the colors of despair. The stories here are not mere fiction; they are the lived experiences of individuals whose voices have been drowned out by the noise of power struggles and the silence of international indifference.

In Chapter III, the narrative delves into the chasm between the dreams that fueled a fierce fight for freedom and the harsh reality of a promise unkept. The tales here speak of a second liberation—a liberation not from an oppressor, but from the shackles of misrule and the specter of a future that seems to slip further away with each passing day.

Chapter IV is a tribute to the valiant, to those who bore arms in the name of liberty only to be forsaken by the very nation they sought to forge. It is a chapter that resonates with the echoes of betrayal and the search for meaning in a landscape that has forgotten the price of its peace.

Finally, Chapter V confronts the reader with the grim tableau of a government's abdication of its most basic duties. It is a chapter that lays bare the consequences of a leadership mired in self-preservation at the cost of its people's well-being.

'The Stolen Nation' is more than a book—it is a testament to the indomitable spirit of the South Sudanese people. It is a call to the world to bear witness to the plight of a nation still in the throes of becoming. As you embark on this journey through the pages of this anthology, may you find not only the stories of a people's struggle but also the undying embers of their hope for a dawn yet to come.

Welcome to 'The Stolen Nation'—a chronicle of dreams deferred but not defeated, a narrative of a nation stolen but still standing, ever defiant in the face of the longest night, waiting for the promise of a new day.

Chapter I

Chapter I of this anthology lays bare the devastating impact of rampant corruption on South Sudan, a nation already grappling with the scars of conflict. The government's institutions, instead of serving the people, have been hijacked by a culture of greed and self-enrichment. The consequences are stark and undeniable: essential services remain woefully inadequate, leaving citizens deprived of basic healthcare, education, and infrastructure. A particularly egregious example of this systemic corruption is the scandalous withholding of diplomats' salaries for three years, a blatant disregard for the service and dedication of those representing the nation abroad.

This corruption manifests in myriad insidious forms, from the illicit exchange of bribes and the unjust taxation of innocent citizens to the shameless diversion of resources intended for the vulnerable into the pockets of the unscrupulous. Land grabbing, the manipulation of legal and administrative systems, and the gross negligence of responsibilities further exacerbate the situation, creating an environment where the rule of law is routinely flouted.

Inflated procurement processes have enriched a select few while depriving the nation of vital resources, further perpetuating the cycle of poverty and despair. This pervasive corruption has eroded public trust in the government, undermined the rule of law, and hindered the country's progress towards stability and prosperity.

Living on a Borrowed Time

The air in the embassy was thick with frustration, a palpable tension that clung to the walls like dust. It had been three years since the last salary, three years of promises and empty assurances from the South Sudanese government. The diplomats now bore the weight of their nation's financial woes on their shoulders.

Aisha, the senior diplomat, stared out the window at the bustling streets of Paris. The city, a kaleidoscope of activity and vibrancy, felt like a cruel mockery of their own desolate reality. Her once-proud bearing was now slumped, her eyes reflecting the exhaustion of constant struggle.

'How can we represent our people when we ourselves are struggling to survive?' she muttered, her voice heavy with despair.

Her colleague, Daniel, a young man with a bright future now clouded by uncertainty, sighed. 'We're living on borrowed time, Aisha. Our savings are depleted, our families are worried, and the government... well, they just don't seem to care.'

Their situation was a microcosm of the larger crisis unfolding in South Sudan. The country, born out of a bloody struggle for independence, was now wrestling with a devastating civil war, economic collapse, and a corrupt government that seemed more interested in self-preservation than the welfare of its people.

The diplomats, once symbols of South Sudan's burgeoning independence, were now reduced to begging for assistance from foreign governments. They were forced to take on second jobs, sell their possessions, and rely on the generosity of friends and family.

One day, a delegation from the South Sudanese government arrived at the embassy. They came bearing promises, but no money. They spoke of reforms, of a brighter future, but their words rang hollow in the ears of the weary diplomats.

'We can't continue like this,' Aisha declared, her voice firm despite the tremor in her hands. 'We need action, not empty words. We need our salaries, we need support, and we need a government that cares about its people.'

The delegation left, their promises echoing in the silent embassy. Aisha and Daniel looked at each other, their eyes filled with a mixture of exhaustion and defiance. They knew the road ahead would be long and difficult, but they were determined to fight for their dignity, their families, and their nation.

Meanwhile in Roman Gai Lel Ngundeng sat huddled against the cold stone wall of the Trevi Fountain, his face buried in his hands. Tears streamed down his cheeks, mingling with the grime of the street. He was homeless, a South Sudanese diplomat, evicted from his apartment by a landlady tired of his government's unpaid rent.

Gai Ngundeng had come to Rome with dreams of representing his young nation, of building bridges between South Sudan and the world. He had arrived with a heart full of hope, a head full of plans, and pockets full of promises. But the promises had turned to dust, the plans to ashes, and the hope to a hollow echo in his chest.

His government, struggling to keep its own people afloat, had failed to send him the funds he needed to pay his rent. Gai Ngundeng had made repeated pleas, sent countless emails, and made desperate calls, but his pleas had fallen on deaf ears. The government, consumed by internal strife and corruption, had forgotten about its diplomats, forgotten about its promises of support.

He watched tourists toss coins into the fountain, their laughter a cruel reminder of his own misfortune. He thought of his family back home, his wife and children, living in a country ravaged by war and poverty. He had left them to serve his nation, only to find himself abandoned by that very nation.

His story was not unique. Gai Ngundeng was just one of many South Sudanese diplomats around the world facing the same plight. They were the forgotten faces of a failed state, forced to live in squalor, their pride and dignity shattered. They were the silent witnesses to the government's negligence, their suffering a testament to the country's broken promises.

Gai Ngundeng knew he couldn't stay on the streets forever. He needed to find a way to survive, to support his family, to rebuild his life. He had to find a way to escape the shadow of his country's failure. But the weight of his situation pressed down on him, a crushing burden of despair.

As the sun began to set, painting the sky in hues of orange and red, Gai Ngundeng looked up at the majestic

Colosseum, a symbol of Rome's ancient glory. He wished he could tell the tourists, the world, the story of his people, the story of their suffering, the story of their desperate hope.

He wished he could tell them that his story, the story of the homeless diplomat, was not just a personal tragedy, but a reflection of a nation in crisis, a nation crying out for help, a nation begging to be remembered.

The diplomats, despite the hardships, continued their work. They held onto the fragile hope of a better future, a future where South Sudan would rise from the ashes and reclaim its place on the world stage. They were a testament to the resilience of the human spirit, a beacon of hope in the darkness, waiting for the day when their government would finally acknowledge their sacrifices and honor their commitment.

A Facilitation Fee

The air in the cramped office was thick with the scent of stale coffee and desperation. A young woman, Ojjaba, sat hunched over a pile of documents, her face etched with worry. She needed a birth certificate for her newborn son, but the clerk, a man with a perpetual frown and a greasy comb tucked behind his ear, kept pushing her paperwork aside.

'Come back tomorrow,' he'd said, his voice flat and emotionless.

Ojjaba knew what he meant. Tomorrow, she'd have to bring him something – a 'facilitation fee', they called it. A bribe. It was an open secret in Juba. Civil servants, struggling to survive on meager salaries, had turned to this unspoken system for survival. They were paid a pittance, barely enough to cover their rent and food, leaving them vulnerable to the lure of easy money.

Ojjaba, a single mother, had no money to spare. She worked as a street vendor, selling fruit and vegetables, barely making ends meet. The birth certificate was crucial for her son's future, for school, for healthcare, for everything. But the system was rigged against her.

Across town, in the gleaming offices of the National Revenue Authority (NRA), a similar scene was unfolding. A businessman, Michael, sat anxiously across from a senior officer, his palms sweating. He had a mountain of paperwork to file, and the officer, a man with a polished smile and a gold watch, was holding him hostage.

'The paperwork is in order,' Michael said, his voice strained. 'I've followed all the regulations.'

The officer smirked. 'Regulations? Regulations are for the poor. For the likes of you, there's a small facilitation fee. Makes things move a little faster, you see.'

Michael, a struggling entrepreneur, knew he had no choice. He had a loan to repay, a business to run. He paid the bribe, his heart sinking with every cent.

This was the reality of South Sudan. A nation rich in oil, but crippled by corruption. The government, plagued by internal strife and economic instability, had failed to provide its civil servants with a living wage. And in the vacuum, a culture of bribery had taken root, slowly poisoning the very fabric of society.

Ojjaba, unable to afford the bribe, watched her son grow older without the legal documentation he needed. Michael, burdened by the cost of corruption, struggled to keep his business afloat. Their stories were a microcosm of the larger tragedy unfolding in South Sudan. A nation yearning for peace and prosperity, held captive by the invisible chains of corruption.

The future, for Ojjaba, Michael, and countless others, remained shrouded in uncertainty. The only hope was that one day, the government would recognize the urgency of the situation, and address the root cause of the problem – the lack of decent salaries for its civil servants. Until then, the cycle of bribery would continue, perpetuating a vicious cycle of poverty and injustice.

The Checkpoint

The dust swirled around Amina's feet, a gritty reminder of the parched earth and the parched lives in South Sudan. She clutched her meager bundle of firewood tighter, her eyes darting nervously. The checkpoint ahead, a rickety wooden structure manned by soldiers with bored expressions and guns slung over their shoulders, was a constant source of anxiety.

Amina knew the drill. The soldiers, their faces obscured by grime and fatigue, would demand a bribe, a 'tax' for her right to pass. Her firewood, her only income, would be judged, and the price would fluctuate depending on their mood, their need, their greed.

Today, she was lucky. The soldier, a young man barely older than her, looked at her with a flicker of pity in his eyes. He waved her through, muttering something about 'poor woman, no money.' Amina felt a surge of relief, her heart a hummingbird in her chest. She had passed, but the feeling of being at the mercy of someone else's whim lingered.

This was the reality of life in South Sudan, a country plagued by the absence of rule of law and the insidious tendrils of corruption. The government, fragile and struggling, had little control over the vast expanse of land. The soldiers, poorly paid and often operating outside the chain of command, were a law unto themselves.

Amina's story was a microcosm of this larger reality. She had seen her neighbors robbed, their livestock stolen, their homes burned down. She had seen justice mocked, replaced by a system where the powerful preyed on the weak.

The lack of justice was a festering wound, fueling the cycle of violence and despair. Trust was a scarce commodity, replaced by suspicion and fear. The very fabric of society was fraying, the threads of hope unraveling.

But Amina, like many others, clung to the hope of a brighter future. She dreamt of a South Sudan where the rule of law prevailed, where corruption was eradicated, and where every citizen had the right to live with dignity and security.

She kept walking, her firewood bundle heavy on her shoulders, but her spirit lighter. She knew that the journey towards justice would be long and arduous, but she had a flicker of hope, a tiny flame that refused to be extinguished. For in the absence of rule of law, the human spirit, though battered and bruised, could still find a way to endure.

A Tale of Deceit

In the heart of South Sudan, a land ravaged by conflict and hunger, a tale of deceit and corruption unfolded. Known as the 'Dura Saga,' it became a symbol of the deep-seated rot that plagued the young nation.

Fearing an impending famine, the South Sudanese government, under the leadership of President Salva Kiir, embarked on an ambitious plan to procure vast quantities of cereals. Amidst the urgency, a staggering sum of nearly $1 billion was paid to 290 firms for deliveries that never materialized.

As the months turned into years, the nation grew restless. The promised cereals, a lifeline for millions, failed to arrive. Instead, rumors of rampant corruption and embezzlement began to circulate. A 2013 report by the Voice of America shed light on the scandal, revealing that not a single grain had been delivered.

World Bank auditors, dispatched to investigate, uncovered a web of deception. They discovered that 290 firms had been paid without ever signing a contract, a blatant violation of procurement protocols. Furthermore, 151 firms were found to have been grossly overpaid, with some receiving as much as 500% more than the market rate.

A criminal probe was launched in the wake of these revelations, seeking to unravel the truth behind the missing cereals and the exorbitant prices paid. Investigators faced an uphill battle, as evidence had been tampered with and key witnesses had disappeared.

One of the central figures in the scandal was a prominent businessman named George. George, who had close ties to the government, was accused of masterminding the scam. He allegedly used fake companies to pocket millions of dollars while leaving the country starving.

As the investigation progressed, a pattern of systemic corruption emerged. Government officials, eager to profit from the crisis, colluded with contractors to inflate prices and pocket kickbacks. The system was rigged, and the people of South Sudan were the ultimate victims.

The Dura Saga became a national shame, exposing the deep-rooted corruption that had infiltrated the highest levels of government. It undermined trust in the administration and further destabilized a country already torn apart by war.

In the end, no individuals were held accountable for the scandal. The stolen millions vanished, never to be recovered. And the people of South Sudan, left to fend for themselves, continued to suffer from hunger and poverty. The Dura Saga served as a grim reminder of the devastating consequences of corruption and the urgent need for accountability and transparency in public life.

A Silent War

The humid air hung heavy over Juba, a pregnant silence broken only by the distant rumble of a generator. Kiden, her brow furrowed in concentration, knelt before a small patch of earth, her fingers meticulously tracing the boundary of her family's plot. It was a struggle, the land parched and cracked, but it was theirs. It was where her grandmother had taught her to plant sorghum, where the scent of her mother's cooking wafted on the breeze, where her father had told stories under the star-strewn sky.

Kiden, like many others in Juba, was fighting a silent war. A war against land grabbers, men with money and influence who saw the city's burgeoning growth as an opportunity to seize land, leaving the original inhabitants with nothing but the bitter taste of displacement. It was a silent war because the land grabbers operated with a chilling efficiency, using their connections to manipulate legal documents and intimidate those who dared to resist.

The whispers started subtly. A neighbor, a well-meaning but desperate man, approached Kiden's family, offering a "better" piece of land, a more lucrative deal, closer to the city's growing infrastructure. The offer was tempting, but it reeked of desperation and a hidden agenda. Kiden's father, a man with calloused hands and a heart hardened by years of struggle, refused. "This land is our legacy," he declared, his voice strong despite the tremor in his hands.

But the whispers turned into threats. The land grabbers, emboldened by their impunity, began to encroach on the boundaries, claiming the land as their own. The local officials, their pockets lined with bribes, offered empty promises of legal protection. Kiden's family, like many others, was caught in a web of deceit and fear.

One scorching afternoon, Kiden watched in horror as a bulldozer, its metal teeth gleaming under the relentless sun, tore through her neighbor's plot. The cries of her neighbor's children, their faces etched with fear, echoed in her ears. They had lost their home, their livelihood, their past. Kiden knew then that she couldn't remain silent.

She started small, sharing her story with others, gathering evidence of the land grabbers' illegal activities. She organized meetings, sparking a fire of defiance in the hearts of her community. They were a diverse group, united by their shared struggle: farmers, shopkeepers, schoolteachers, all grappling with the threat of losing their homes and their dreams.

The fight was uphill. The land grabbers had power, money, and connections. But Kiden and her community had something more: courage. They were willing to stand up for their rights, to fight for their heritage, to reclaim their stolen land. They knew that the battle wasn't just about land, it was about their identity, their future, their very survival.

The community organized protests, their voices rising in a chorus of defiance. They approached the media, exposing the land grabbers' corrupt practices. They filed legal challenges, armed with the evidence they had painstakingly gathered. The fight was long and arduous, but their resilience slowly began to chip away at the land grabbers' power.

One day, a small victory arrived. The local court, pressured by the mounting evidence and the community's unwavering determination, ruled in favor of Kiden's family and several others. It was a small victory, but it was a sign of hope, a beacon of light in the darkness.

Kiden stood on her family's plot, the soil still bare but alive with possibility. She looked at the faces around her, etched with hardship but shining with a newfound strength. They had fought for their land, and in doing so, they had fought for their dignity, their community, their future. The fight was far from over, but they had learned that even in the face of overwhelming odds, the power of unity and courage could move mountains, even in the heart of a city grappling with the injustice of land grabbing.

A Bitter Pill of Complicity

Aya's stomach churned as she stared at the ragged figures huddled at the gate. They were just children, barely teenagers, their faces etched with the weariness of a life lived on the streets. Their eyes, though, held a spark of defiance, a flicker of hope that seemed to pierce through the layers of despair. She knew their story, the story of a nation ravaged by war, a nation where the children were the first victims.

She was a cog in the machinery of the South Sudanese government, a cog that had become tarnished with the grease of corruption. For years, she had turned a blind eye, swallowed the bitter pill of complicity, justifying her actions as a means to survive. But today, the sight of these children, their skeletal frames a testament to the nation's suffering, had shattered the illusion.

Aya worked in the Ministry of Finance and Planning, a fortress of power and privilege. She knew the system, the loopholes, the hidden accounts where the stolen wealth of the nation was stashed. The money, the lifeblood of the country, was being siphoned off, leaving behind a trail of poverty and despair.

'Shall I return the money I looted to the country?' she whispered, the question echoing in the silent chamber of her heart. The thought was terrifying, a monstrous beast waiting to devour her. The regime, ruthless and unforgiving, would crush anyone who dared to defy its iron grip. Corruption was the norm, a venomous vine that had wrapped itself around the entire system, suffocating any hope of change.

But the image of the children, their hollow eyes mirroring the hollowness of her own soul, haunted her. She saw the reflection of her own complicity in their suffering. 'How can I live with myself?' she thought, the question a sharp blade twisting in her gut.

The answer came in a whisper, a voice she had buried deep within: 'You can't.'

The decision was made. She wouldn't be another nameless face in the crowd, another cog in the machine of corruption. She would fight, even if it meant risking everything. She would expose the truth, even if it meant facing the wrath of the regime.

The journey was fraught with danger. She knew the price she might pay, but she was determined to pay it. She started small, leaving anonymous tips to journalists, leaking documents to international organizations. It was a slow, meticulous process, each step a gamble, each move a brush with death.

The regime retaliated, its iron fist tightening. Aya was followed, her phone tapped, her every move monitored. But she refused to back down. She had tasted the bitter fruit of corruption, and she knew the sweetness of redemption.

One day, a news report flashed across the screen, revealing the hidden accounts, the names of the corrupt officials, the magnitude of the theft. The news spread like wildfire, igniting a spark of hope in the hearts of the people. It was a small victory, a tiny crack in the wall of corruption, but it was enough.

Aya knew she had made a difference. The children at the gate, their faces no longer etched with despair but with a glimmer of hope, were a testament to her sacrifice.

She had returned the stolen money, not to the country, but to the people, to the children who deserved a better future. She had faced the wrath of the regime and survived, not unscathed, but with her soul intact. She had chosen the path of redemption, and in doing so, she had found her own salvation.

A Ghost Shell

The humid South Sudanese air hung heavy, thick with the scent of dust and simmering resentment. Nyanjur, the Minister of Health, sat in her air-conditioned office, the plush carpet muffling the insistent cries of the sick outside. Her phone buzzed, a notification from her private bank account - a tidy sum had just landed, a quarterly dividend from her offshore investments. The money was more than enough to buy a new car, maybe even a luxury villa in Dubai. But the thought brought no joy.

Nyanjur glanced at the worn-out photograph on her desk; a young girl, her eyes wide with hope, holding a tattered book. It was a photo of her younger self, taken before the war, before the corruption, before the money. Her stomach churned with a guilt she couldn't ignore. Her ministry, the very institution meant to serve the people of South Sudan, was crumbling. The hospitals were ghost shells, lacking basic supplies, the doctors disillusioned and underpaid. The people, especially the children, were dying.

Every day, Nyanjur witnessed the stark contrast: the opulence of her life and the crushing poverty of her people. She knew the reason for the disparity. Her ministry, like every other government institution in South Sudan, was a breeding ground for corruption. The funds meant for hospitals and medicines were diverted, siphoned away by officials like her, leaving behind a trail of despair.

Nyanjur had started with good intentions. She genuinely wanted to help her people. But the system was rigged. The war had left the country vulnerable, its institutions weak, and the corrupt officials had taken advantage. Nyanjur had succumbed to the pressure, accepting bribes, turning a blind eye to the embezzlement, all for the sake of survival, for the sake of her family. She justified it, telling herself she was using the money to help people in other ways, to fund small clinics in the villages, to sponsor struggling students. But she knew it wasn't enough. The guilt was a constant, gnawing presence, a reminder of her betrayal.

One day, a delegation of doctors arrived from abroad, eager to help. They brought with them a mountain of supplies, enough to equip a hospital, enough to save lives. But they were aghast at the state of the ministry, the utter lack of infrastructure, the blatant corruption. They threatened to leave, their mission deemed futile.

Nyanjur looked at the doctors, their faces etched with disgust, and saw a reflection of her own shame. She realized she could no longer live with the hypocrisy. The money meant nothing in the face of the suffering she was responsible for.

That night, Nyanjur made a decision. She called a meeting with the other officials, her voice shaking as she confessed her guilt, her complicity. She revealed the truth about the stolen funds, the corruption that had crippled their ministry. The room was silent, the air thick with tension.

The road ahead was uncertain. But Nyanjur knew she had to try, to fight for the people she had failed for so long. She knew it would be a long and arduous journey, a struggle against a system deeply entrenched in corruption. But she had to start somewhere, to atone for her sins, to reclaim her humanity. She had to try to heal the wounds she had inflicted, not just on her people, but on her own soul.

The photo of her younger self on her desk seemed to smile, a faint glimmer of hope in her eyes. Nyanjur knew she had a long way to go, but she was finally ready to walk the path towards redemption.

A Gnawing Sense of Disillusionment.

The sun beat down on the cracked earth, baking the air and turning the dust into a shimmering haze. It was a scene that had become all too familiar to Kacuol, who sat on a rock by the roadside, watching the occasional car kick up a cloud of dust as it rattled past. The Bahr El Ghazal Road, a ribbon of concrete that was supposed to connect the South Sudanese capital, Juba, to the mineral-rich region of Bahr El Ghazal, was a monument to unfulfilled promises.

Launched with fanfare in 2015, the road had been touted as a symbol of progress, a lifeline for the war-torn nation. The government had boasted that the road would boost trade, improve transportation, and bring prosperity to the region. But nine years later, the road was a mere shadow of its intended glory. The tarmacked stretch barely reached 30 kilometers, a pathetic testament to the project's failure.

Kacuol, like many others, had watched the road's progress with a mixture of hope and skepticism. He had witnessed the initial enthusiasm, the flurry of activity as construction crews moved in, the promises of a brighter future. But as the years went by and the road remained unfinished, his hope dwindled, replaced by a gnawing sense of disillusionment.

The road had become a metaphor for the state of the nation – riddled with corruption, hampered by conflict, and plagued by a lack of accountability. The concrete stretches, like broken teeth, stood as a grim reminder of the government's failures.

One day, a government official arrived, a polished politician with a well-rehearsed speech about the road's progress and the benefits it would bring. Kacuol listened, his face a mask of skepticism. He saw the official's well-tailored suit, the expensive car, the air of confidence, and he felt a surge of anger.

'Where is the progress?' he demanded, his voice hoarse from the dust. 'Where are the benefits? All we see is broken promises and unfinished roads.'

The official, caught off guard by Kacuol's outburst, stammered, offering a string of excuses. But Kacuol wasn't interested in excuses. He had seen too many broken promises, witnessed too much suffering. He was tired of waiting for a future that never seemed to come.

As the official retreated, defeated, Kacuol looked at the road, the concrete evidence of failed promises. He knew that the road might never be completed, that the journey to progress was long and arduous. But he also knew that he wouldn't give up hope. He and his fellow South Sudanese would keep fighting for a better future, even if it meant paving their own way, one small step at a time.

A Toxic Brew of Despair

The sun beat down on Juba, a relentless furnace baking the city and its people. A young man named Wani, barely 20, sat on a dusty street corner, his face etched with the weariness of hopelessness. He held a tattered diploma, a testament to years of hard work and a dream of contributing to his nation, South Sudan. But the dream was slowly dying, choked by the suffocating grip of nepotism.

Wani had graduated top of his class in Civil Engineering. He had hoped to join the public service to help rebuild his war-torn country. But the doors remained firmly shut. Every position was filled by a relative, a friend, or a crony of someone in power. Wani watched as unqualified individuals were appointed to crucial roles, their only qualification being their connection to someone in the inner circle.

The consequences were devastating. Roads crumbled, bridges collapsed, and vital infrastructure projects stalled. The country, already struggling to recover from years of civil war, was further crippled by the incompetence of those appointed through nepotism. Corruption flourished, diverting funds meant for development into the pockets of the privileged few.

Wani wasn't alone. Thousands of young, talented South Sudanese like him were left jobless, their skills wasted. The frustration and anger simmered, turning into a toxic brew of despair. The dream of a united and prosperous

South Sudan, so hard-won, was fading under the weight of nepotism.

One day, Wani stumbled upon a group of young people gathering in a dusty courtyard. They were discussing ways to fight the rampant corruption and nepotism. They were tired of being ignored, of seeing their nation crumble while the elite prospered. Wani felt a flicker of hope. He joined the group, his voice adding to the chorus of discontent.

Together, they organized peaceful protests, demanding accountability and transparency. They raised awareness about the devastating impact of nepotism, using social media and local newspapers to spread their message.

Their voices, though small at first, began to echo across the country, resonating with others who had suffered under the weight of corruption.

The government, initially dismissive, was forced to acknowledge the growing movement. It was a long and arduous struggle, filled with threats and intimidation. But the young people persevered, fueled by their belief in a better future for South Sudan.

Slowly, the tide began to turn. The government, facing mounting pressure, reluctantly began to implement reforms. The media, emboldened by the public outcry, started reporting on corruption and nepotism with greater scrutiny.

Wani, along with his fellow activists, continued to fight for change. They knew the road ahead was long and difficult, but they were no longer alone. The seeds of hope, planted by their unwavering commitment, were starting to sprout. They believed that one day, South Sudan would rise above the shadows of nepotism, and become the nation it was meant to be: a land of opportunity and prosperity for all.

Chapter II

Chapter II of this anthology delves into the devastating consequences of South Sudan's government's negligence, painting a stark picture of a nation struggling to survive. The government's blatant disregard for environmental safety has led to rampant oil pollution, contaminating rivers, land, and ultimately, the people who rely on these resources for their survival. This environmental devastation is compounded by the government's failure to provide basic security for its citizens. In both urban areas and rural communities, a lack of protection has allowed for the emergence of various militias, who terrorize villages, destroy livelihoods, kill innocent people, and abduct women and children. The government's own security forces are not exempt from these atrocities, and the forceful disappearance of government critics, including activists, journalists, and politicians, further underscores the climate of fear and repression. This lack of security and accountability is mirrored in the government's failure to provide essential services. Healthcare, education, infrastructure, and protection of civilians are all woefully inadequate, leaving the population vulnerable and desperate.

The government's inability to pay civil servants and organized forces decent salaries on time highlights the systemic corruption and mismanagement that permeates every level of society. This chapter paints a harrowing portrait of a nation struggling under the weight of its own government's incompetence and indifference, leaving its people to face the brutal reality of a broken system.

A Life Sucked Out of the Land

The air hung heavy with the smell of oil and decay. A pungent, oily mist clung to the leaves of the few remaining trees, their branches skeletal against the harsh, sun-baked sky. This was the reality of South Sudan, where the oil boom had brought not prosperity, but a slow, suffocating death.

Akuch, a young woman with eyes as dark as the oil that stained the earth, knelt beside a shallow well. Her hands, calloused from years of labor, scooped up the murky water. It was this water, poisoned by the oil spills and toxic runoff, that her family drank. 'Mama,' she whispered, her voice choked with despair, 'this water is killing us.'

Akuch's father, a weathered man with a face etched with the harshness of the land, nodded grimly. He remembered when the oil companies arrived, promising jobs and prosperity. They had built their rigs, their machinery churning the land, their promises echoing in the air. But the promises were hollow. The land, once fertile, was now barren. The water, once clear, was now contaminated. The air, once fresh, was now thick with the stench of oil.

Akuch's father was one of the many who had lost their livelihood, their land seized by the oil companies. They had become 'oil refugees', forced to live on the fringes of the oil fields, their lives poisoned by the very resource that promised them wealth.

Akuch's gaze drifted to the horizon, where the oil rigs stood like monstrous sentinels, spewing smoke into the sky. A sense of injustice burned in her. The oil companies, with their vast resources, had done this to her people, to her land. They had polluted their water, poisoned their air, and left them to suffer.

But Akuch was not one to sit idly by and watch her people die. She'd heard whispers of a group, a coalition of activists and lawyers, who were fighting to hold the oil companies accountable for the damage they had caused. They were called the 'Oil Justice Warriors', and they were determined to bring the polluters to justice.

Akuch knew the risks. The South Sudanese government, heavily reliant on oil revenue, was complicit in the environmental destruction. They had neglected environmental and safety regulations, turning a blind eye to the suffering of their own people. But Akuch was not afraid. She had seen the suffering in her own family, in her own community. She had seen the life sucked out of the land, the hope drained from the eyes of her people.

She knew she had to fight. For her family, for her community, for the future of South Sudan. She knew the fight would be long and arduous, but she was determined to join the Oil Justice Warriors and fight for their right to clean water, clean air, and a future free from the toxic legacy of oil.

The struggle was long and fraught with danger. Akuch faced threats, intimidation, and even imprisonment. But she persevered, her spirit fueled by the hope of a cleaner, healthier future for her people. Her story, like the stories of countless others, became a testament to the resilience of the human spirit, a testament to the power of hope in the face of environmental devastation.

The fight for oil justice in South Sudan continues. The journey is long, the path is treacherous, but Akuch and the Oil Justice Warriors are determined to hold the oil companies accountable, to reclaim their land, and to breathe life back into the land that was stolen from them. Because for them, the fight is not just about oil, it's about their survival, their dignity, their future. It's about reclaiming their home, their land, their lives. It's about fighting for a future where the air is clean, the water is pure, and the land is fertile once again.

A Squeezed Political Space

The dust swirled around Hanan's feet, kicking up a reddish-brown cloud that mirrored the anger churning in her stomach. The once vibrant marketplace, bustling with life and the cacophony of bartering, was eerily quiet. The only sounds were the mournful wind whistling through the skeletal remains of stalls, and the distant, muffled cries of children.

Hanan had been a weaver, her nimble fingers transforming vibrant threads into intricate patterns that adorned the lives of her community. But the vibrant tapestry of her life was shredded, ripped apart by the relentless hand of political turmoil. The government had tightened its grip on every aspect of life, squeezing the air out of civic spaces.

The market, once a hub of free exchange, had become a ghost town. The government, in its quest for control, had choked the life out of it, forcing vendors to pay exorbitant fees, and silencing any whispers of dissent. Hanan's loom, once a symbol of her independence, now stood silent, a testament to the stifled freedom.

Her son, Omar, a bright young man with a hunger for knowledge, had dreamed of studying in the capital. But the university, once a beacon of hope, had become a ground for wasting time as lecturers find it difficult to come to the campus to deliver lectures due to lack of transport money. Omar's dreams were crushed, replaced by a gnawing sense of helplessness.

The once vibrant community gatherings, where people shared stories and laughter, were replaced by hushed whispers and fear. The government security had infiltrated these spaces too, using informants and threats to stifle any form of independent thought. Even the church, a sanctuary of solace, was not immune. Sermons were carefully crafted to praise the government, and whispers of dissent were met with suspicion.

Hanan felt the weight of the suffocating grip of the government on every facet of her life. The policy of the government was to control, to silence, to erase any vestige of independent thought. But Hanan, like many others, refused to be silenced. She clung to the fading memories of a vibrant community, of a time when freedom was a shared breath.

One evening, under the cloak of darkness, Hanan gathered a small group of friends. Their faces were etched with worry, yet their eyes held a spark of defiance. They spoke in hushed tones, sharing stories of oppression, of dreams stifled, of lives choked by fear. They agreed, their voices barely a whisper, to fight back, to reclaim their stolen freedoms.

Hanan knew it was a dangerous path, but she also knew that silence was not an option. The future of her community, the dreams of her son, the very essence of their lives, depended on their courage. In the face of the suffocating grip of the government, they would weave a new tapestry, thread by thread, a tapestry of hope, resilience, and the unwavering belief in the power of a free spirit.

A Terrorized Village.

The sun beat down on the parched earth, baking the dust into a fine, choking powder. Aluel, a young girl of twelve, sat huddled in the shade of a mango tree, clutching her younger brother, Omot, to her chest. The air was thick with the smell of fear and smoke.

Just yesterday, their village had been a haven of laughter and life. Now, it lay in ruins, a charred testament to the brutal reality of South Sudan. The raiders, men with faces painted in the colors of war, had come in the dead of night, their guns spitting fire and hate. They had stolen their cattle, their food, their hope. Aluel watched, numb, as her father's body was dragged away, his face contorted in pain.

Omot whimpered, 'Aluel, are we going to die?'

She squeezed him tighter, whispering, 'No, Omot. We're going to be okay. We'll find Mama.'

But the truth gnawed at her. Their mother had been taken too, along with the other women. Aluel knew that they would be sold into slavery, their lives reduced to a cruel parody of what they once were.

Driven by a desperate hope, Aluel started walking, her feet heavy with grief and exhaustion. She had no idea where she was going, but she had to keep moving. Omot, small and fragile, clung to her, his eyes reflecting the fear that gnawed at her own heart.

They stumbled through the unforgiving landscape, dodging the occasional stray bullet and the hostile stares of men carrying weapons. They scavenged for scraps of food, sharing them sparingly. Every rustle in the bush, every shadow, sent chills down their spines.

One day, they came across a small, dusty village. The people were wary, their faces etched with the same pain Aluel carried within her. But they were kind, offering them food and a place to rest.

Aluel learned that the raiders were not just cattle thieves, but a group of men driven by hatred and fueled by the insatiable hunger for power. They had been waging a bloody war for years, leaving a trail of destruction and broken lives in their wake.

Aluel knew that her journey was far from over. She had to find her mother, even if it meant crossing the border, venturing into the unknown. She had to find a way to bring peace to a land that seemed eternally trapped in a cycle of violence.

As the sun dipped below the horizon, casting long shadows across the parched earth, Aluel looked at Omot, his face smeared with tears and dirt. She knew that their journey was just beginning. It would be long and arduous, filled with danger and uncertainty. But she would not give up hope. Not for Omot, not for her mother, not for their stolen future.

In the heart of a land ravaged by war, a young girl's resilience and love shone like a beacon of hope, a testament to the enduring spirit of humanity.

Vanished Without a Trace

In the war-torn land of South Sudan, where ethnic conflicts and political unrest had ravaged the nation for years, a sinister plot unfolded in the shadows. The government, led by an iron-fisted regime, sought to silence any voice that dared to challenge its authority.

Amidst the chaos and bloodshed, innocent civilians vanished without a trace. Families were torn apart, friends disappeared overnight, leaving behind a chilling void. The government denied any wrongdoing, claiming it was 'unknown gunmen.' But behind the facade of order, a dark secret lurked.

One such victim was Mel, a young journalist who had courageously exposed corruption and human rights abuses. His articles had sparked outrage among the populace, but they had also drawn the ire of the authorities. One fateful night, Mel was forcibly abducted from his home. His screams were swallowed by the darkness as he was dragged into a waiting vehicle.

As days turned into weeks, Mel's family desperately searched for him, pleading with officials for answers. But their pleas fell on deaf ears. The government remained silent, its agents disappearing into the labyrinthine bureaucracy. Mel's disappearance became a chilling message to other dissenters: speak out, and you will face the same fate.

Meanwhile, in a secret detention center in the capital, Mel was subjected to unspeakable horrors. He was tortured, interrogated, and denied any contact with the outside world. His resolve wavered as he faced the relentless brutality, but a flicker of hope remained within him.

Through a network of underground activists, word of Mel's ordeal reached the international community. Human rights groups and foreign governments condemned the government's actions, demanding his immediate release. Pressure mounted, and the regime was forced to make a decision.

In a desperate attempt to appease the growing outrage, the government announced Mel's 'release.' However, he was not the same man who had been abducted. His body was bruised and broken, his spirit shattered. He was released as a warning, a living testament to the consequences of speaking out.

Mel's story became a symbol of the countless other innocent civilians who had been forcibly disappeared in South Sudan. Their voices had been silenced, their lives extinguished in the government's ruthless pursuit of control. And as the instability raged on, the sinister scheme of eliminating dissent voices continued, casting a long and dark shadow over the nation's future.

A Sealed Fate

In the desolate and war-torn land of South Sudan, healthcare had become a distant dream. The government, plagued by corruption and instability, had long abandoned its people, leaving them to fend for themselves in the face of unimaginable suffering.

Poni, a young mother of three, clung desperately to her frail child, her heart heavy with despair. Little Pagan had been battling malaria for days, but the nearest clinic was hours away and utterly unequipped. With each passing hour, Pagan's fever raged higher, his body wracked by relentless chills.

Poni knew she had to seek help, but the journey was perilous. Armed militias roamed the countryside, and the roads were flooded, almost impassable. Yet, driven by a mother's desperation, she embarked on the treacherous path.

As she walked, Poni's thoughts drifted back to the days when South Sudan had been a glimmer of hope. After decades of civil war, independence had brought the promise of a better future. But the dream had been shattered by mismanagement, violence, and neglect.

The healthcare system had crumbled into ruin. Hospitals stood empty, their walls crumbling, and equipment stolen. Medical supplies were scarce, and trained professionals had fled the country. The few remaining healthcare workers struggled tirelessly, but they were overwhelmed and underpaid.

As Poni approached the clinic, her heart sank. The building was a dilapidated shack, its windows shattered and its roof leaking. Inside, a single nurse struggled to tend to a crowd of sick and injured patients. There were no beds, no medicines, and no hope.

Poni watched in horror as the nurse turned her away, unable to help Pagan. Desperation surged through her veins as she realized that her child's fate was sealed. In that moment, the true extent of South Sudan's healthcare nightmare became all too clear.

Night after night, Poni cradled Pagan in her arms, her heart shattering with each passing hour. As the fever consumed her child, Poni whispered prayers and sang lullabies, desperate to ease his suffering.

In the end, Pagan was one of countless victims of South Sudan's healthcare crisis. His death was a testament to the government's failure, the corruption that had stolen his future, and the cruel neglect that had condemned him to a life of misery.

A Darkness of Insecurity

In the heart of East Africa, where the scorching sun beat relentlessly upon the parched land, lay South Sudan, a nation gripped by a nightmarish reality. Neglected by its government, the country had descended into a maelstrom of violence and insecurity.

Nyibol, a young woman from a remote village, had witnessed firsthand the horrors that plagued her homeland. Militia groups roamed the countryside, wreaking havoc and leaving behind a trail of destruction. Government forces, ill-equipped and underfunded, struggled to maintain order.

Night after night, Nyibol would lie awake, her body trembling with fear as the sounds of gunfire echoed through the darkness. The walls of her hut seemed to close in on her, suffocating her with the weight of her worries. Her mind raced, conjuring up images of her loved ones being torn from her embrace.

One fateful night, as the stars twinkled mockingly above, Nyibol's worst nightmare came to life. A band of militiamen stormed her village, their machetes glinting in the moonlight. Chaos erupted as they looted homes, set fires, and slaughtered innocent civilians.

Amidst the carnage, Nyibol's parents were ruthlessly murdered before her very eyes. Their screams of anguish haunted her every waking moment, a constant reminder of the horrors she had endured.

As the militiamen retreated, leaving behind a smoldering ruin, Nyibol stumbled through the wreckage, her heart broken and her spirit shattered. She had lost everything—her family, her home, and any semblance of safety.

With nowhere to turn, Nyibol wandered aimlessly, her body weak and her mind numb. She became a refugee in her own country, living on the fringes of society, forgotten by the government that had failed to protect her.

As the years passed, South Sudan's nightmare continued unabated. The government remained paralyzed by corruption and incompetence, while the people suffered in silence. Nyibol's story became a grim testament to the devastating consequences of a nation abandoned to its fate.

And so, in the desolate wasteland that was South Sudan, the darkness of insecurity prevailed, casting a long shadow over the lives of its people, who lived in a perpetual state of nightmares.

A Voice of Dissent

The humid air hung heavy, thick with the scent of dust and fear. Keji, her eyes shadowed by worry, watched the men in their faded uniforms converge on the village. They were the 'Peacekeepers', the government soldiers sent to maintain order, but their arrival brought no peace. They came with their guns and their promises, promises whispered in hushed tones, promises laced with lies.

Keji's husband, Samuel, was a village elder, respected for his wisdom and integrity. He had refused to bend to the government's demands, refusing to join their militia and denounce the rebels. For the government, this made him a threat, a voice of dissent, and a target.

The soldiers, led by a man called John Luka, approached their hut with the practiced ease of predators. They spoke of reconciliation, of a unified South Sudan, their words dripping with honeyed deceit. They promised protection, but their eyes held the glint of wolves.

'Your husband is a valuable asset to our cause,' John Luka declared, his voice oily smooth. 'He can help us bring stability to this land.'

Keji knew the truth. They wanted Samuel to be their puppet, to use his influence to sway the villagers. They wanted him to betray his people, to turn against everything he believed in.

'He will not betray his people,' Keji stated, her voice firm despite the tremor in her heart. 'He will not join your militia.'

John Luka's smile turned predatory. 'He will,' he said, his voice low and dangerous. 'Or your village will face the consequences.'

Days turned into weeks, a slow, agonizing spiral of fear. The soldiers harassed the villagers, stealing their livestock, burning their crops. They spread rumors, sowing seeds of discord and suspicion. They held Samuel captive, using him as a bargaining chip, a constant reminder of their power.

One night, under the watchful eyes of the moon, John Luka visited Keji. He offered a deal, a twisted bargain. He would release Samuel if she agreed to speak against the rebels, to spread their propaganda. He knew her love for her husband was her weakness, her Achilles' heel.

Keji, her heart torn apart, faced a terrible choice. Betray her beliefs, her husband's principles, and save him? Or hold onto her integrity and watch him perish?

The weight of the decision crushed her. She looked at the soldiers, their faces masks of menace, and then at the faces of her neighbors, etched with fear and despair. She knew the government's promises were empty, their 'peace' a cruel facade.

"I will not betray my people," she said, her voice trembling but unwavering.

John Luka's smile was a chilling thing, a predator's victory. He turned and left, leaving Keji with the chilling certainty of Samuel's fate.

The next morning, Samuel's body was found in the forest, his face a mask of pain, a testament to the cruel reality of South Sudanese politics.

Keji, her heart shattered, knew that the lies, the deceit, and the manipulation would continue. The fight for peace and justice would be long and arduous. But she also knew that the truth, like a seed buried deep in the earth, could not be extinguished. It would sprout, defying the darkness, and one day, perhaps, it would bloom.

A Tapestry of Broken Promises.

The sun beat down on the parched earth, baking the dust into a fine, suffocating powder. Elizabeth, her face etched with the weariness of a thousand sunrises, sat on the cracked concrete stoop of her home, her gaze fixed on the sprawling cityscape beyond.

'It's not the South Sudan I want,' she muttered, her voice a low growl against the relentless heat. The words, a constant refrain in her mind, spilled out in a torrent of frustration.

Elizabeth, a young woman with a fire in her eyes and a thirst for justice, had dreamt of a South Sudan free from the shackles of war, a land where her children could grow up in peace and prosperity. But the reality was far from her utopian vision.

The city, a testament to the country's nascent independence, was a tapestry of broken promises. Potholes scarred the roads, buildings stood unfinished, and the air hung heavy with the stench of corruption. The government, riddled with infighting and incompetence, seemed more interested in enriching itself than serving its people.

'Imbeciles,' she spat, her voice laced with bitterness. 'They own the state, not the people.'

Elizabeth wasn't alone in her disillusionment. The whispers of discontent, like the wind through the dry grass, rustled through the city. People spoke of nepotism, of stolen funds, of opportunities squandered. The anger simmered beneath the surface, a volatile mix of frustration and despair.

Elizabeth, however, refused to be consumed by despair. She had a responsibility, a duty to her community, to her children. She had to fight for the South Sudan she dreamt of, the South Sudan she knew was possible.

She joined a group of activists, their meetings held in hushed tones, their plans meticulously crafted. They knew the risks, the potential for violence, but they were willing to take the chance, to stand up for what they believed in.

They organized peaceful protests, their voices rising in unison, demanding accountability, demanding change. They circulated pamphlets, exposing the corruption that choked the nation. They used the power of the internet, their message spreading like wildfire.

The authorities, however, were quick to react. Their response was brutal, their tactics ruthless. Activists were arrested, their voices silenced. The fear, a suffocating blanket, threatened to smother the movement.

But Elizabeth refused to be intimidated. Her anger, fueled by the injustice she witnessed, burned brighter than ever. She knew that the struggle for a better South Sudan was not a sprint, but a marathon, one that would require immense courage and unwavering determination.

'We will not be silenced,' she declared, her voice ringing with defiance. 'This is our country, and we will fight for it, even if it takes our lives.'

And so, the fight continued, a relentless struggle against the tide of corruption and despair. The South Sudan Elizabeth dreamt of might seem distant, but she refused to give up hope. For in her heart, she knew that the spirit of her people, their resilience and their yearning for a better future, would ultimately prevail.

An Opulent Feast

In the heart of Juba, the capital of South Sudan, a nation plagued by poverty and conflict, a stark contrast emerged. While the government proclaimed an austere budget amidst widespread economic hardship, a lavish celebration unfolded for a different occasion.

As the sun dipped below the horizon, casting a golden glow over the city, the streets surrounding the presidential palace were adorned with twinkling lights and vibrant banners. The air crackled with anticipation as crowds gathered to witness the endorsement ceremony for Salva Kiir, the incumbent president.

Inside the grand ballroom, a glittering assemblage of ministers and generals sipped champagne and dined on an opulent feast. The walls were draped in crimson velvet, and crystal chandeliers sparkled overhead. The atmosphere was one of unrestrained extravagance.

'We have come together tonight to celebrate a momentous occasion,' declared Kiir, his voice booming over the sound system. 'The endorsement of my candidacy is a testament to the confidence that our people have in my leadership.'

As the president spoke, a murmur of discontent rippled through the crowd. Outside, on the impoverished streets, ordinary South Sudanese struggled to make ends meet.

The country was teetering on the brink of famine, and essential services were woefully inadequate.

'This celebration is a mockery,' whispered Nyamal, a young woman who had come to the city in search of a better life. 'They say they have no money for our schools or hospitals, but they can spend it on these lavish parties.'

Her words echoed the sentiments of many South Sudanese, who felt betrayed by their leaders. The government had repeatedly failed to provide basic necessities, while squandering public funds on personal enrichment and lavish displays.

As the endorsement ceremony drew to a close, the crowd dispersed into the night. The lights dimmed, and the music faded away. But the contrast between the opulence within the palace walls and the poverty outside remained stark and unforgiving.

For the people of South Sudan, the celebration of Kiir's candidacy endorsement was a bitter reminder of the broken promises and missed opportunities that had plagued their country for far too long. It was a symbol of the deep-seated inequality and corruption that had hindered their progress and stolen their dreams.

Chapter III

Chapter III of this anthology delves into the stark reality of broken promises that have haunted South Sudan since its independence. The liberation that was fought for with such fervor has yielded a bitter truth: the government's rampant corruption has plunged the nation into a cycle of misery. Citizens, once filled with hope, now question the very existence of their independent state, their dreams of prosperity shattered by the harsh realities of hunger, disease, illiteracy, and a lack of development.

Despite abundant resources, the leadership of President Salva Kiir has failed to translate potential into tangible benefits for the people, leaving them clinging to an elusive prosperity that seems perpetually out of reach. A second liberation, a yearning for a true realization of the ideals that fueled the first struggle for independence, has taken root in the hearts of citizens.

This Chapter III lays bare the consequences of government negligence – a collapsed economy, a breakdown of the rule of law, a dearth of employment opportunities, and a population reliant on humanitarian aid for basic survival, including the provision of food. The once-celebrated independence has become a hollow victory, a stark reminder of the chasm between lofty aspirations and the harsh realities of a nation grappling with its own failings.

An Elusive Prosperity

The sun dipped below the horizon, painting the dusty plains of South Sudan in hues of crimson and gold. A lone figure, weathered and stooped, sat by a sputtering fire, its flames reflecting in his tired, gray eyes. He was Ajang, a veteran of the long and bloody struggle for South Sudan's independence. He had fought for freedom, for a better life, for his children. But now, staring at the meager meal of dried beans, a question gnawed at his heart.

'What did I fight for?' he rasped, his voice hoarse from years of dust and hardship.

His daughter, Aken, a young girl with eyes as bright as the fire, looked up from her own bowl. She had heard this question before, countless times. It hung in the air like a shroud of despair, a reminder of the harsh reality that followed their hard-won freedom.

'You fought for us, Baba,' she said, her voice small but firm. 'You fought for a South Sudan where we could live in peace, where we could go to school, where we could have food on the table.'

Ajang's heart ached. He had fought for a future where his children wouldn't have to survive on dry beans, where they could learn and dream. But the reality was far from that. The war had left scars on the land, on the people, and on him. The promised prosperity had been elusive, replaced by poverty, corruption, and a gnawing sense of disillusionment.

'But look at us, Aken,' he said, his voice choked with emotion. 'We live in a shack, we have no land, no work. What peace is there? What freedom?'

Aken's eyes, though young, held a wisdom beyond her years. 'We have each other, Baba,' she said, her hand reaching out to touch his. 'We have hope. We have a future.'

Ajang looked at her, at the firelight dancing in her eyes, and a flicker of hope ignited within him. He had fought for a future, for his children, and even though that future seemed far away, it wasn't lost. His daughter, with her unwavering spirit, reminded him that even in the midst of hardship, there was still a reason to fight, a reason to believe.

He took her hand, his own weathered fingers trembling slightly. 'You are right, Aken,' he said, his voice stronger now, a flicker of determination in his eyes. 'We have each other. We have hope. And we will find a way. We will build a better future, for you, for all of us.'

The future was uncertain, but Ajang knew one thing for sure: he wasn't done fighting. He had fought for freedom, for a better tomorrow, and he would continue to fight, not just for himself, but for his daughter, for the future of South Sudan, for the dream he had fought so hard to achieve.

Living by Humanitarian Food

The sun, a harsh, unforgiving orb, beat down on the parched earth, turning the dust into a swirling, choking haze. A thin, skeletal woman, her face etched with the hardship of countless sunrises, knelt beside a meager pile of grain. Her name was Abuk, and she was one of the millions in South Sudan who lived on the razor-thin edge of survival, teetering on the precipice of famine.

Abuk had once been a farmer, her land a vibrant tapestry of green, her days filled with the satisfying labor of tending to crops. But that was before the rains failed, turning her fertile fields into cracked, parched earth. The war, a constant, gnawing presence, had swallowed her husband, leaving Abuk to navigate the treacherous landscape of hunger and despair alone.

The government, a distant, uncaring entity, had become a phantom in the lives of people like Abuk. Promises of aid were whispered like windblown dust, vanishing as quickly as they came. The meager rations provided by humanitarian organizations, a lifeline thrown from a distant shore, were the only thing standing between Abuk and starvation.

Each day, Abuk woke with a gnawing emptiness in her stomach, a constant reminder of her precarious existence. The grain, carefully measured and rationed, was her only source of sustenance. She would grind it into a coarse flour, mixing it with water to form a thin, tasteless porridge. It was barely enough to keep her alive, but it was all she had.

One day, a group of children, their eyes hollowed with hunger, approached Abuk. They were her neighbors, their families struggling like hers. Abuk shared her meager meal with them, her heart aching at their desperation. She knew that even this small act of generosity would leave her with less for herself, but she couldn't stand to see the children suffer.

As she watched them eat, a flicker of anger ignited within her. Why should they have to depend on the charity of others? Why did the government, the supposed protectors of their land, turn a blind eye to their plight?

Abuk's anger was not a mindless rage, but a burning desire for justice. She knew that the government, with its vast resources, could do more to help. She knew that they could provide seeds, tools, and training to help the farmers recover from the dry spell. She knew that they could build infrastructure to improve the lives of their people. She knew that government would improve the security and protect the people.

But the government remained indifferent, its focus seemingly elsewhere, leaving millions like Abuk to fend for themselves.

One day, a group of aid workers arrived, their faces etched with concern. They spoke of the looming famine, of the dire need for food and medical supplies. They promised to help, to bring relief to those in need.

Abuk listened intently, her heart filled with a mixture of hope and skepticism. She had heard these promises before, only to see them fade into the dust of broken promises. But this time, there was something different in the eyes of the aid workers, a genuine sense of urgency, a deep commitment to helping.

As the aid workers began distributing food and supplies, Abuk felt a glimmer of hope ignite within her. Maybe, just maybe, things would be different this time. Maybe the government would finally be forced to acknowledge their plight, to take responsibility for the well-being of their people.

But as the sun dipped below the horizon, casting long shadows across the parched earth, Abuk knew that the fight for survival was far from over. The road ahead was long and arduous, and the future remained uncertain. But she held onto the hope that, one day, the government would finally hear the cries of its people and fulfill its responsibility to provide them with the basic necessities of life.

For now, Abuk would continue to live on the edge, surviving on humanitarian aid, her spirit unbroken, her hope flickering like a candle in the wind. She knew that the fight for a better life was not over, and she would continue to fight, for herself, for her children, and for all those who had been forgotten.

A Hollow Victory

The dust swirled around Achol's feet, a reddish-brown cloud that mirrored the anger in her heart. Ten years ago, she had dreamt of a South Sudan free from the tyranny of the North, a land where her children could live in peace. Now, she stood in the shadow of the crumbling market, its stalls looted and burned, watching the remnants of her life turn to ash.

The dream of independence had turned into a nightmare. The government, riddled with corruption and infighting, had failed to provide even the most basic necessities. Roads were impassable, healthcare was a luxury, and the only constants were the ever-present hunger and the fear of violence.

Achol's village was just one of many that had been ravaged by the endless cycle of tribal clashes. The government, too weak to provide security, had become a spectator to the rise of militias. These groups, fueled by desperation and tribal loyalties, filled the power vacuum, dispensing their own brand of justice with brutal efficiency.

Achol's son, Daniel, had joined one of these militias. He had told her it was the only way to protect their family, to ensure they wouldn't be the next victims. He had promised to bring peace, but the rage in his eyes when he spoke of the atrocities committed by rival militias chilled Achol's soul.

The militias were a symptom of the government's failure, a grotesque parody of the very freedom they had fought for. They preyed on the vulnerable, their leaders enriching themselves while the people they claimed to protect suffered. Achol had seen the militiamen steal cattle, burn villages, and disappear women. The whispers of their brutality echoed in every corner of the land.

One day, a group of militiamen stormed her village. They demanded food and supplies, their faces masked by dust and the shadow of their own savagery. Achol, her heart pounding, watched as they looted her meager belongings, their eyes gleaming with a hunger that went beyond the physical.

As they left, a young militiaman, his face etched with a chilling mixture of fear and cruelty, looked at her. He was barely older than her son, his eyes reflecting the same emptiness that had consumed Daniel.

'This is the new world,' he said, his voice raspy with the dust of the battlefield. 'This is the only way to survive.'

Achol stared at him, her heart breaking. The dream of a free South Sudan had become a cruel joke, a hollow victory that had given birth to a new kind of oppression. The militias, fueled by the government's failure, had become the new masters of this broken land, their reign of terror a chilling testament to the price of a shattered dream.

As she watched the militiamen disappear into the dust, Achol knew that the fight for a better future was far from over. But the path ahead was shrouded in uncertainty, the air thick with the stench of fear and despair. The future of South Sudan, like the dust that swirled around her, was uncertain, a bleak landscape where the only constant was the struggle for survival.

The Whispers of Discontent

The dust swirled around Mary's feet, a gritty reminder of the parched earth, a parched land, a parched hope. She clutched her youngest child, his skinny limbs trembling against her worn blouse. The child, barely two, whimpered, his eyes mirroring the hopelessness that had settled over the nation like a shroud.

Mary had lived through the war, the bloody struggle for independence. Now, in the supposed peace, the hunger gnawed at their bellies, a constant companion. Her husband, a farmer, had lost his land to floods, another consequence of the erratic weather patterns, a consequence of the neglect that had gripped the nation since independence.

'Where is the promised peace?' she muttered, her voice a dry rasp. The answer, a bitter echo in her heart, was the man they called Salva Kiir. A man who had led them to freedom, only to lead them into a new kind of slavery. A slavery of corruption, of power struggles, of a government that seemed more interested in enriching itself than in caring for its people.

The stories were whispered in hushed tones, tales of stolen wealth, of oil fields exploited, of the government's coffers overflowing while the people starved. Mary had seen it firsthand, the crumbling infrastructure, the lack of basic services, the whispers of discontent brewing in the hearts of her people.

One day, a group of young men, their faces etched with anger and desperation, gathered in the dusty square. They spoke of their dreams, shattered by the reality of their existence. They spoke of the leaders who had promised a better life, only to deliver a life of despair. They spoke of the need for change, for a new dawn, a new leadership.

Mary listened, her heart stirring with a flicker of hope. The young men, fueled by their passion, were a beacon in the darkness. They were the spark that could ignite the fire of change, a fire that could burn away the corruption and bring a true peace to their land.

She watched as the men marched, their voices rising in a chorus of discontent, a chorus that echoed Mary's own silent plea. Their march was a testament to the resilience of the human spirit, a reminder that even in the darkest of times, hope could bloom.

Mary, holding her child close, knew that the road ahead would be long and arduous. But she also knew that the people of South Sudan, with their unwavering spirit, would not be broken. They would fight for their future, for their children's future, for a better tomorrow.

The nightmare of Salva Kiir's leadership may have seemed insurmountable, but Mary, and the millions like her, knew that even the darkest night can be overcome by the dawn of a new day. They would fight for that dawn, for a South Sudan where the children could laugh without fear, where the land could flourish again, where the promise of peace could finally be realized.

A Victim of a Broken Nation

The dust of the long journey clung to Anyijong like a second skin. Five years. Five years he had spent in the cramped, echoing anonymity of a Nairobi slum, working twelve hours a day in a textile factory for a pittance. Five years he had dreamt of returning home, of the lush green fields of his childhood, of the warm embrace of his family. He had convinced himself that time would have brought change, that the economic situation in South Sudan would have improved.

The bus coughed its way into Juba, a city choked by the same dust that clung to Anyijong. The air was thick with the stench of poverty and despair. The streets were clogged with beggars, their hands outstretched, their eyes hollowed by hunger. The vibrant city he remembered was gone, replaced by a shell, a ghost town of broken dreams.

His heart sank as he navigated the familiar streets, each one a painful reminder of what had been lost. The once bustling market was a desolate wasteland, the stalls empty, the vendors gone. The school where he had learned his ABCD was now a crumbling ruin, its windows shattered, its walls graffitied with the pain of a nation.

He found his family huddled in their mud-brick home, their faces etched with the same despair that haunted the city. His mother, her eyes red-rimmed, embraced him, but her touch was cold, devoid of the warmth he remembered. His father, once a proud farmer, sat hunched, his hands shaking, his eyes filled with a terrible emptiness.

Days turned into weeks, and the harsh reality of South Sudan settled upon Anyijong like a suffocating blanket. The economic situation was worse than he had imagined. The currency was worthless, food was scarce, and the violence that had driven him away had only intensified. He saw the desperation in the eyes of his fellow citizens, the longing for a life they could no longer afford.

The dream he had carried for five years, the dream of returning home, of rebuilding his life, of finding solace in the familiar embrace of his homeland, crumbled before his eyes. He was trapped, a prisoner of circumstance, a victim of a broken nation.

One evening, sitting by the flickering light of a kerosene lamp, Anyijong listened to his father speak. His voice was raspy, his words filled with a profound sadness. 'Anyijong,' he said, 'We are living in a nightmare. We are losing our children, our land, our future. We are losing hope.'

Anyijong looked at his father, his face etched with pain, and he knew he had to do something. He couldn't stay, couldn't watch his family, his nation, slowly wither away. He would have to leave again, not as a refugee, but as a fighter, a beacon of hope, a testament to the resilience of the human spirit. He would leave, but he would return, and when he did, he would bring with him the strength to rebuild, the courage to fight, the unwavering belief in the future of South Sudan.

A Gnawing Stomach

The sun beat down on Juba, a city choked by dust and despair. Akol, a young police officer, sat slumped against a wall, his stomach gnawing with hunger. It had been nine months since he'd last received a salary. His family, back in the village, were relying on him, yet he couldn't even afford a loaf of bread.

'Another day, another empty pocket,' he muttered, watching a convoy of Landcruiser SUVs speed past, their tinted windows obscuring the faces of the elite within. Those vehicles, he knew, were filled with stolen money, the lifeblood of the kleptocratic regime that ruled South Sudan.

Akol remembered the day the news broke. The government, in a move that shocked even the most hardened cynics, had announced the suspension of salaries increment for all civil servants and organized forces. The official reason? A 'temporary financial shortfall.' Akol, like many others, knew the truth: the money was being siphoned off, funneled into the pockets of corrupt officials and their cronies.

The streets of Juba were a reflection of the nation's plight. Market stalls were deserted, their owners too weak from hunger to even try to sell their wares. Children, their eyes hollowed by malnutrition, wandered aimlessly, their innocence tainted by the harsh realities of their world.

Akol, though weary, refused to succumb to despair. He joined a group of disgruntled police officers who were organizing a protest. They met with their commander and demanded their salaries.

Their protest was not received lightly. The police leader used force and arrested Akol with his colleague. Akol watched in horror as his comrades were beaten. He, too, was captured and thrown into the notorious Juba Central Prison.

Inside the prison, he found himself surrounded by fellow civil servants, teachers, doctors, and soldiers, all victims of the regime's greed. They shared their stories, their anger, their desperation. Yet, even in the darkest of times, hope flickered.

Akol, inspired by the resilience of his fellow prisoners, refused to give up. He knew that the fight for a better South Sudan was far from over. He would continue to fight, not just for himself, but for his family, his nation, and the future of a people who had suffered enough.

A Thousand Lost Dreams

The wind whipped through the cracked window of the makeshift classroom, carrying with it the dust of a forgotten land. Inside, 12-year-old Biong sat hunched over a worn textbook, the pages brittle and faded. The teacher, a young woman with eyes that held the weight of a thousand lost dreams, struggled to maintain order amidst the chaos. Hunger gnawed at Biong's stomach, but the gnawing of despair was far worse.

South Sudan, a land born from the ashes of war, was now a land of broken promises. The government, consumed by its own struggles, had forgotten the children. Education, the lifeline to a better future, was left to wither like a neglected field.

Biong's school was a testament to this neglect. The building, once a symbol of hope, was now a crumbling shell. The walls, once painted with vibrant murals, were now scarred with the graffiti of despair. The roof leaked during the rainy season, forcing the children to huddle under plastic sheets, their faces reflecting the gloom of the sky.

The textbooks were scarce, handed down like precious heirlooms. The desks were rickety, barely able to hold the weight of the children's dreams. The teachers, underpaid and overworked, were forced to juggle multiple subjects, their passion slowly fading with each passing day.

Biong's nightmare began long before the classroom. It started with the walk to school, a perilous journey through a land ravaged by conflict. Hunger gnawed at his insides, a constant companion on his journey. He had seen things that no child should ever see, the scars of war etched into the landscape and the faces of his people.

The nightmare continued in the classroom, where the lessons were a blur, the words fading into the background noise of his aching stomach and the whispers of his own despair. He had learned to dream in whispers, his ambitions a faint echo in the desolate landscape of his reality.

His dream, like a fragile flower struggling to bloom in the desert, was of a school with a roof that didn't leak, with books that were new and desks that were strong. He dreamt of a teacher who could teach him without the burden of hunger and despair. He dreamt of a South Sudan where education was not a privilege, but a right, where children were not forgotten, but nurtured.

But the nightmare was real, and it threatened to consume him. He looked at the teacher, her eyes filled with a flicker of hope, and he knew that the fight for education, for a better future, was a fight they had to win, together.

One day, Biong woke up from a nightmare, but this time, it wasn't the same. He saw a glimmer of light, a flicker of hope in the darkness. It was a vision of a new South Sudan, a land where children were not forgotten, where education was not a nightmare, but a promise. And in that promise, he found the strength to fight, to keep dreaming, to keep believing in a better tomorrow.

A Wasteland of Hunger

The wind whipped across the parched earth, carrying the scent of dust and despair. Monica, her ribs showing beneath her thin cotton dress, clutched her emaciated son, Deng, closer. He whimpered; his tiny body wracked with hunger. Her heart ached, a dull, heavy ache that mirrored the emptiness in her stomach. The last sorghum had been eaten days ago.

Monica had heard whispers of government aid, of trucks filled with grain, but they had never reached their village. The government, preoccupied with its own struggles, seemed to have forgotten them, these people clinging to life on the dusty plains of South Sudan. The whispers, like the wind, carried their hopes away, leaving them stranded in a wasteland of hunger.

At night, Monica dreamt of food. Mountains of grain, ripe and golden, stretched before her. She reached out to grasp a handful, but her fingers closed on dust. The grain shimmered and dissolved, leaving her with a gnawing emptiness.

Deng, too, dreamt of food. In his dreams, he saw a plump, white bread, soft and fragrant. He reached for it, but it slipped through his fingers, leaving him with a taste of ash on his tongue.

The days blurred into weeks, each one a slow, agonizing crawl towards oblivion. Monica watched her son weaken, his eyes losing their sparkle, his laughter replaced by whimpers. The government's neglect was a silent, suffocating presence, a shroud of despair that threatened to engulf them.

One day, a flicker of hope appeared on the horizon. A group of aid workers, their faces etched with concern, arrived in their village. They brought with them bags of grain, their arrival a beacon of light in the encroaching darkness.

Monica, her eyes brimming with tears, watched as the workers distributed the food. She held Deng close, his tiny body trembling with hunger. As she fed him the precious grain, she felt a sliver of hope rekindle within her. The government might have forgotten them, but the world, it seemed, had not.

The dream of mountains of grain remained, but now it was tinged with a flicker of hope. The nightmare of hunger, though still present, was no longer so absolute. The world, she knew, was vast and complex. But even in the darkest of times, a single act of kindness, a single grain of rice, could make a difference. And in that difference, she saw a glimmer of a future, a future where her son, and all the children of South Sudan, could dream of a life free from hunger.

A Breeding Ground for Chaos

In the desolate heart of South Sudan, where the sun blazed relentlessly and the land lay parched, a nightmare unfolded. The government, a phantom entity absent from the daily struggles of its people, had abandoned them to a cruel fate.

Amidst the crumbling infrastructure and shattered dreams, Ajok, a young woman with a heart heavy with despair, fought to survive. Her once vibrant village was now a ghost town, its inhabitants scattered by conflict and neglect.

As the sun dipped below the horizon, casting long shadows across the barren landscape, Ajok huddled in her makeshift shelter. The walls, once a source of comfort, now offered little protection from the elements or the relentless torment of her thoughts.

Memories of a distant past, when laughter and hope filled the air, haunted her. Now, only silence and desperation clung to her like a suffocating blanket. The government had become a cruel mirage, its promises of peace and prosperity nothing but empty echoes.

With each passing day, the nightmares intensified. Ajok would awake in a cold sweat, her heart pounding with terror. She saw visions of abandoned hospitals, where the sick and dying lay unattended. She witnessed the destruction of schools, leaving children with no future but the horrors of war.

The government's neglect had left South Sudan a breeding ground for chaos. Armed groups roamed freely, terrorizing civilians with impunity. The rule of law had collapsed, replaced by a reign of violence and lawlessness.

As the darkness descended, Ajok's fears transformed into a terrifying reality. A group of armed men stormed her village, their faces twisted with malice. They pillaged and burned, leaving behind nothing but smoldering ruins.

In the aftermath of the attack, Ajok stood alone amidst the wreckage. Her world had been shattered once more, her dreams reduced to dust. The government's neglect had not only destroyed her home but had also extinguished the last flicker of hope within her.

As the sun rose on another day, casting a cruel light on the devastation, Ajok's heart filled with a profound sense of despair. South Sudan, once a land of promise, had descended into a living nightmare. And as the government remained silent, the country's stability crumbled, leaving its people trapped in an endless cycle of suffering and despair.

The Brewing Storm

The air crackled with anticipation in the stadium. Thousands of people, their faces painted in the SPLM colors, chanted the candidate's name – a roar that echoed across the dusty plains of the capital. A sea of flags, banners, and posters swayed in the heat, a testament to the party's deep pockets. But beneath the surface of the vibrant display, a silent unease simmered.

Nyanut, a young teacher, stood amongst the crowd, her heart heavy. The cheers seemed to mock the empty cupboards in her home, the unpaid bills piling up. Her salary, like that of countless other civil servants and soldiers, had been delayed for 9 months. The government, she knew, had diverted funds meant for their wages to finance the extravagant rallies, each more opulent than the last.

This wasn't the first time. The cycle was all too familiar: promises of a better future, lavish campaigns, and then, the same old story of neglect and corruption.

Nyanut wasn't alone. In the shadows, whispers of discontent grew louder. Soldiers, their families starving, began to question their loyalty. Doctors, nurses, and teachers, their morale shattered, contemplated leaving their posts. The fabric of the nation, already frayed by years of conflict, threatened to unravel.

The candidate, basking in the adulation of the crowd, remained oblivious to the brewing storm. His speeches, filled with hollow promises and empty platitudes, were met with a growing sense of cynicism.

The candidate, his face now pale with fear, realized the gravity of the situation. The echoes of the crowd's cheers were replaced by the deafening roar of a nation on the brink of collapse.

The story of the SPLM presidential candidate's campaign, a tale of lavish spending and neglect, served as a stark reminder that true leadership demanded more than just empty promises and political grandstanding. It demanded accountability, empathy, and a genuine commitment to the welfare of the people. The people, after all, were not just voters, but the very foundation upon which a nation stood.

A Graveyard of Dreams

The wind whipped across the parched earth, carrying with it the scent of dust and desperation. Betty, her face etched with the weariness of a thousand sunrises, clutched her youngest child close. Her other two, gaunt and silent, trailed behind, their eyes reflecting the same bleak emptiness that mirrored her own. They were walking, as they had been for days, towards the horizon, a shimmering mirage of hope.

South Sudan, their home, had become a graveyard of dreams. The government, a distant, uncaring entity, had failed them. The land, once fertile and bountiful, was now a wasteland, ravaged by years of conflict and neglect. The rains had failed, leaving their crops to wither and die. The wells had run dry, forcing them to trek miles for a meager sip of water. The promise of peace, a fragile whisper in the wind, had long since faded into the dust.

Betty had seen her village crumble, its once vibrant life reduced to a ghost town. She had watched her neighbors, her friends, succumb to hunger and disease. She had buried her husband, his life snuffed out by the violence that had become their constant companion. Now, she was left with nothing but the tattered remnants of her family and a desperate hope for survival.

Their journey was arduous, a slow, agonizing crawl towards the border. The sun beat down mercilessly, turning the earth into a shimmering furnace. Hunger gnawed at their bellies, their bodies growing weaker with each passing day. But they kept walking, driven by a primal instinct to survive, to find a place where their children could have a chance.

The border, a barely visible line in the dust, was a beacon of hope. Beyond it lay Uganda, a land rumored to offer refuge and a chance at a new life. As they crossed, Betty felt a weight lift from her shoulders, a sliver of hope flickering in her heart.

But the journey was far from over. The refugee camp, a sprawling city of tents, was a testament to the sheer scale of South Sudan's tragedy. Thousands had come before them, their faces etched with the same weariness, the same desperate hope.

Betty knew that their struggle was far from over. The scars of war and neglect would take time to heal, the memories of loss would linger. But for now, she had a roof over her children's heads, a warm meal in their bellies, and a glimmer of hope for a future beyond the dust and despair of South Sudan.

The refugee camps, a testament to the government's failure, were a constant reminder of the tragedy unfolding in South Sudan. Each new arrival, each weary face, was a story of lost dreams, of lives shattered by neglect and violence. Betty, and countless others like her, had become refugees, a stark reminder of the human cost of a government that had failed its people.

Chapter IV

Chapter IV of this anthology delves into the stark reality of broken promises that have come to define the post-independence South Sudan. It lays bare the chasm between the dream of a prosperous nation and the grim reality of a government that has seemingly forgotten its core commitments. The narrative focuses on the plight of the SPLA veterans, the very individuals who fought tirelessly for liberation, only to find themselves betrayed by the government they helped create.

This Chapter IV poignantly depicts the veterans' struggle to reconcile their unwavering belief in the dream of freedom with the harsh realities of neglect and disillusionment. It explores the profound sense of betrayal they experience as they grapple with the question of what they fought for, their sacrifice seemingly rendered meaningless by a government that has failed to deliver on its promises.

The Chapter IV delves into the intricate web of government negligence, exposing how the veterans, who risked their lives for a brighter future, are now left to navigate a system that seems determined to deny them the very benefits they deserve. The narrative becomes a poignant testament to the fragility of hope, highlighting the devastating consequences of broken promises and the enduring struggle to find meaning in a reality that falls far short of the dreams that fueled the liberation struggle.

A Broken Promise

The wind whipped across the parched earth, carrying the scent of dust and despair. Ruben, his weathered face etched with the pain of a thousand forgotten promises, sat perched on a rock overlooking the desolate landscape. This was his land, his home, but it felt like a stranger now, ravaged by war, its beauty obscured by the scars of conflict.

His mind drifted back to the day they had fought for freedom. The young, idealistic Ruben, brimming with hope, had joined the rebellion, fueled by the promise of a brighter future for his people. He had seen comrades fall, witnessed unspeakable atrocities, all for the dream of a South Sudan free from the shackles of oppression.

The day they achieved independence, the joy was palpable, a wave of euphoria washing over the nation. Ruben had felt it too, a surge of hope that his sacrifices had not been in vain. They had finally tasted freedom, the bitter fruit of their struggle.

But the taste was short-lived. The euphoria faded, replaced by a slow, agonizing realization that the promised paradise was a mirage. The leaders, once revered heroes, became entangled in power struggles, their promises of unity and prosperity dissolving into a bitter brew of tribalism and corruption.

The land, once fertile and vibrant, withered under the weight of neglect. The scars of war, instead of healing, festered, erupting into new cycles of violence. Ruben watched, his heart heavy with disillusionment, as the dream he had fought for crumbled before his eyes.

He had been a young man, full of faith, when he had left his village to join the rebellion. Now, his hair was streaked with grey, his youthful idealism replaced by a weary cynicism. The broken promise, the failure of South Sudan's liberation, had become a heavy weight on his soul.

He looked at the sun setting over the horizon, casting long shadows across the desolate landscape. The sky, once a canvas of hope, now reflected the bleak reality of his shattered dream. Ruben knew that the fight for freedom wasn't over, but the fire in his heart had dimmed, replaced by a deep, abiding sorrow. He had fought for a better future, but the future he had fought for had become a cruel parody of his hopes.

And as the dust settled, carrying with it the whispers of a broken promise, Ruben felt a deep sense of loss, a lament for a dream that had turned to ashes. He knew, in the depths of his soul, that the fight for South Sudan's true liberation had only just begun, a fight that would require a new generation of dreamers, a generation that could pick up the pieces of a shattered promise and rebuild a future worthy of the sacrifice.

A Whisper on the Wind.

The sun, a molten disc in the dusty sky, beat down on the makeshift camp, turning the parched earth to shimmering sand. Nyilang, his uniform faded and torn, sat hunched over, his face a mask of weariness. He stared at the cracked earth, the memory of the lush fields of his childhood a distant, bittersweet dream.

Nyilang had fought for his country, for the liberation that had promised a brighter future. But the future had turned into a desert, as harsh and unforgiving as the landscape he now called home. The promise of peace, of prosperity, had been swallowed by the dust of neglect.

His comrades, men who had fought by his side, sat around him, their eyes reflecting the same despair. They were shadows of their former selves, their bodies weakened by hunger, their spirits crushed by the crushing weight of disillusionment. Their uniforms, once symbols of their struggle, were now tattered rags, a testament to the forgotten promises.

Nyilang remembered the day they had marched into Juba, the capital city, a wave of jubilation sweeping across the land. They had tasted victory, felt the thrill of freedom. But the victory was short-lived. The promised infrastructure remained a mirage, the promised jobs a whisper on the wind. The land, once fertile, had turned barren, the crops withered under the relentless sun. The people, their hopes dashed, were left to fend for themselves, their dreams turning to dust.

The soldiers, neglected by the very government they had fought to establish, were left to their own devices. They had become forgotten warriors, their stories lost in the endless expanse of the desert. They were shadows, remnants of a war that had promised so much and delivered so little.

One day, a young soldier, his face etched with a youthful naiveté, approached Nyilang. His eyes, though filled with longing, held a flicker of hope.

'Nyilang,' he said, his voice barely a whisper, 'Tell me, will things ever get better?'

Nyilang looked into the young soldier's eyes, seeing a reflection of his own lost dreams. He sighed, the sound echoing through the desolate camp.

'I don't know,' he said, his voice rough with despair. 'But we must keep fighting, even if it's just for the hope that things might change.'

The young soldier nodded, his eyes filled with a determination that brought a flicker of hope into Nyilang's heart. Perhaps, even in the face of such overwhelming despair, there was still a glimmer of light, a chance for the land, and its people, to rise from the ashes of neglect. Perhaps, one day, the desert would bloom again.

A Forgotten Legion

The humid air hung thick and heavy, clinging to the sweat-soaked clothes of the men gathered around the makeshift fire. A chorus of coughs, ragged and dry, punctuated the silence. They were heroes, these men, veterans of the South Sudanese liberation struggle. They had fought for their freedom, for their land, for their right to exist. Now, they were forgotten, their wounds both physical and emotional, festering in neglect.

Jok, a young man with eyes that held the weight of a thousand battles, sat amongst them. His leg, mangled by a stray bullet, was a constant reminder of the war's brutality. He had been a fierce fighter, a sniper who had taken down countless enemy soldiers. Now, he was reduced to a burden, dependent on the charity of others.

Next to him sat Wol, his face etched with pain. He had lost his eyesight during a fierce clash, his world forever shrouded in darkness. He used to be a renowned strategist, a leader who inspired his men. Now, he was a ghost, lost in a world he could no longer see.

Othom, once a fearless soldier, now bore the scars of a shattered limb. He had fought valiantly alongside his comrades, shedding blood for the promise of a brighter tomorrow. But as the guns fell silent, his dreams crumbled into dust. Discharged from the army, he was left to fend for himself, abandoned in a nation that had turned its back on its former warriors.

Tut, a nurse who had risked his life tending to fallen soldiers, had witnessed the horrors of war firsthand. But upon his return home, he found himself cast aside, his skills and sacrifices deemed worthless. The government, consumed by political strife, had forgotten the sacrifices of its veterans.

Across the fire, sat Lubajo, his body riddled with shrapnel. He was a former soldier, a man of strength and courage. But the war had broken him, leaving him haunted by nightmares and consumed by a constant, gnawing pain. He was a shadow of his former self, his spirit slowly fading with each passing day.

The fire crackled, casting flickering shadows on their faces. They were all victims of a war they had fought to win. Their sacrifices had been forgotten; their stories relegated to dusty archives. The government in power had no concept of the horrors they had endured.

Jok looked at the sky, his gaze lost in the distant stars. He thought of the promises made, the hopes that had fueled their fight. The war had ended, but for them, the struggle continued, a silent battle against despair and neglect.

The Paradox of Liberation

The wind whipped across the parched earth, carrying with it the scent of dust and the whispers of a broken dream. A lone figure, weathered and worn, sat beneath the skeletal branches of a baobab tree. His name was Alier, and he was watching the sun dip below the horizon, a fiery orange ball sinking into the endless expanse of the savanna. The setting sun, he thought, mirroring the fading hope of his people.

Alier had fought in the Second Sudanese Civil War, a young man brimming with the idealism that had fueled the SPLM, the Sudan People's Liberation Movement. He believed in the promise of liberation, of a South Sudan free from the shackles of Khartoum. He had seen comrades fall, tasted the bitterness of defeat, and finally, tasted the sweet nectar of victory. South Sudan was born, a nation built on the ashes of war and the blood of martyrs.

But the dream, Alier realized, was a mirage, shimmering in the heat of the moment. The land, scarred by conflict, was now plagued by corruption, ethnic tensions, and a gnawing hunger. The SPLM, the very movement that had delivered them from oppression, had become their oppressor. The leaders, once revered as liberators, now hoarded power, their pockets lined with oil money while the people struggled to survive.

Alier remembered the words of his grandfather, a wise old man who had seen the rise and fall of empires.

'Liberation,' the old man had said, 'is not just about breaking free from chains, but about building something better. It is a journey, not a destination.' A journey that South Sudan, it seemed, had lost its way on.

He looked at the children playing, their innocent laughter echoing in the twilight. They were the future, the hope for a better tomorrow. But could they truly be free, Alier wondered, when their birthright was a legacy of war and broken promises?

Alier closed his eyes, the familiar ache of disillusionment rising in his chest. The SPLM, he realized, was an illusion, a shimmering mirage in the desert of hope. The paradox of South Sudan's liberation was that it had only brought them to the precipice of a new struggle, a struggle against the very forces that had promised their freedom.

As the stars began to appear, Alier knew he had a choice to make. He could wallow in despair, or he could pick up the pieces of the shattered dream and try to rebuild it, brick by broken brick. He could become part of the solution, not the problem. He could be the change he wished to see in the world, even if it meant facing the ghosts of the past and the demons of the present.

He stood up, the weight of his past and the burden of his future pressing down on his shoulders. He was just one man, a grain of sand in the vast expanse of the savanna.

But even a single grain, he knew, could help shift the sands of time, could help shape a new future for his children, for his people, for his nation. The journey to liberation, he realized, had just begun.

Chapter V

Chapter V of this anthology exposes the abysmal failure of the South Sudanese government to fulfill its fundamental obligations to its citizens. Instead of providing essential services such as healthcare, education, and infrastructure, the government has allowed sycophancy and corruption to flourish. The infamous 'oil for road' scheme exemplifies the rampant corruption that has plagued the country, with government officials enriching themselves while the citizens remain impoverished. President Salva Kiir's lack of political will to implement meaningful change has further exacerbated the situation.

The presale of crude oil, illegal government borrowing, and clandestine corruption have drained South Sudan's coffers, leaving the country vulnerable to economic collapse. The government's use of propaganda and threats through the Ministry of Information and Communication has stifled dissent and silenced critical voices. Meanwhile, the ruling party, the Sudan People's Liberation Movement (SPLM), has infiltrated public institutions, including the Political Parties Council (PPC), undermining the independence of these bodies.

Blinded by Greed and Power

In the heart of East Africa, where the Nile flows through ancient lands, lay the troubled nation of South Sudan. For decades, the country had been ravaged by civil war, corruption, and tribal strife. Amidst this chaos, a sinister force had taken root: governance failure and the insidious rise of sycophancy.

Once expected to be a beacon of hope, South Sudan's government had become a haven for the corrupt and the incompetent leaders, blinded by greed and power, neglected their responsibilities and plundered the country's resources. The rule of law crumbled, replaced by a culture of impunity and patronage.

In this toxic environment, sycophancy flourished like a parasitic vine. Individuals, seeking to curry favor and advance their own ambitions, surrounded themselves with flatterers and yes-men. They whispered sweet nothings into the ears of their superiors, praising their every action and turning a blind eye to their misdeeds.

One such sycophant was Gatkuoth, a young and ambitious politician. With a silver tongue and a knack for self-promotion, he quickly rose through the ranks, becoming an advisor to the president. Gatkuoth's loyalty was unwavering, regardless of the president's questionable decisions. He defended every policy, no matter how harmful, and painted the president as a visionary leader.

As Gatkuoth's influence grew, so did the culture of sycophancy. Critics were silenced or marginalized, while those who spoke out against corruption and mismanagement were branded as traitors. The media became a tool of propaganda, spreading only the government's sanitized version of events.

The consequences of governance failure and sycophancy were devastating. Public services collapsed, leaving millions without access to basic healthcare and education. The economy faltered, as investment fled the country and poverty deepened. Rebellion erupted as citizens grew weary of the rampant corruption and injustice.

Yet, amidst the turmoil, the sycophants remained unscathed. They continued to bask in the reflected glory of their patrons, enjoying lavish lifestyles and immunity from accountability. The country descended into a state of moral bankruptcy, where the pursuit of personal gain trumped all other considerations.

In the end, South Sudan became a cautionary tale about the dangers of governance failure and the corrosive effects of sycophancy. The dream of a prosperous and just nation had been shattered, replaced by a dystopian nightmare where the few preyed on the many. And as the country sank deeper into the abyss, the sycophants whispered sweet nothings, oblivious to the destruction they had wrought.

The Curse of the Unknown

The air hung thick with the scent of desperation and dust in Juba, the capital of South Sudan. It was the rainy season, yet the parched earth refused to drink, the sky a perpetual grey canvas. The fields lay barren, the cattle gaunt, and the people, their faces etched with worry, spoke in hushed tones of famine.

It had been a year since the rains had failed, and with each passing day, the whispers grew louder. The blame, like the dust, settled on an unnamed, faceless entity. 'It's the curse of the unknown,' they said, their eyes wide with fear. 'Someone is using dark magic, a powerful sorcerer, to steal our rain.'

The whispers reached the ears of President Salva Kiir Mayardit, and a shiver ran down his spine. He had faced many challenges in his time as leader, but this, this was different. He had seen the fear in the eyes of his people, felt the desperation in the air. He knew he had to do something, anything, to appease the unseen force.

He called a meeting of his advisors, his voice strained. 'We must find this sorcerer,' he declared, his eyes blazing with a mixture of fear and resolve. 'We must appease him, offer him anything, anything to bring the rain back.'

The advisors, accustomed to navigating the treacherous waters of South Sudanese politics, were hesitant. 'But your Excellency,' one ventured, 'how do we find someone we know nothing about?'

The president's gaze swept over them, his voice a low growl. 'We will find him,' he promised, his words echoing the desperation in his heart. 'We will find him, even if it takes the last drop of water in this land.'

And so began the search. The president announced a nationwide reward for any information leading to the capture of the 'rain-stealing sorcerer.' The streets buzzed with rumors, whispers turning to accusations, fingers pointed at witches, warlocks, and even the president's political rivals.

The president, desperate and increasingly paranoid, became a prisoner of his own palace, his once-powerful presence now shrouded in fear. He offered prayers, sacrifices, and even, in a moment of utter desperation, a portion of his own blood to the unseen force.

But the rain stayed away. The people, their faith in their leader dwindling, started to murmur. 'The president is the sorcerer,' they whispered, their voices barely a breath. 'He is using his power to drain the land, to keep us weak and reliant on him.'

The president, surrounded by his dwindling circle of advisors, felt the ground shift beneath his feet. The whispers had become a chorus, a tide of discontent rising against him. He knew he had to do something, but what?

His eyes fell on a faded photograph on his desk – a picture of him, years ago, standing before a group of children, his face beaming with hope. A memory flickered in his mind – a time when he was not a leader, but a father, a brother, a friend.

He took a deep breath, his heart pounding in his chest. He knew what he had to do. He called for a press conference, his voice trembling, but his eyes strong.

'My people,' he said, his voice raw with emotion. 'We have been looking for a sorcerer, a villain. But the truth is, the villain is not some unseen force, but ourselves. We have been fighting among ourselves, destroying our land, polluting our rivers, and neglecting our resources. We have been the curse upon ourselves.'

The silence that followed was deafening. The president, his voice filled with sorrow, continued. 'I, Salva Kiir Mayardit, take full responsibility for the failure to address the issues that have led to this crisis. I have been blinded by power, by fear, and by my own ambition. I have failed you, my people.'

He spoke of unity, of the need to rebuild their nation, and of the importance of protecting their land. He spoke of the need to work together, to heal the wounds of their past, and to build a future for their children.

The people listened, their faces etched with a mixture of disbelief and hope. The president, for the first time in a long time, felt a glimmer of hope. He had lost his power, his position, perhaps even his future, but he had found something even more valuable – the truth, and the chance to rebuild.

The rain came, not as a miracle, but as a sign of hope, a testament to the power of truth and unity. The land, though scarred, began to heal, the people, though weary, began to smile. The curse of the unknown had been lifted, not by the capture of a sorcerer, but by the courage of a leader who had dared to face his own demons.

The Towering Mountain of Debt

In the heart of the African continent, where the Nile's waters flow through the vast savannah, lay the young nation of South Sudan. Its history was etched with the scars of conflict and the promise of a brighter future. But beneath the surface of hope lurked a sinister secret that threatened to consume the nation's soul.

The government, led by President Salva Kiir, found itself trapped in a quagmire of debt. Years of civil war had drained its coffers, leaving behind a towering mountain of unpaid loans. Desperate for cash, the leaders devised a cunning scheme that would mortgage the future of their people for their own personal gain.

They sold off the nation's oil reserves, the lifeblood of its economy. Foreign corporations were granted exclusive rights to extract and export the black gold, in exchange for upfront payments that filled the government's coffers. The money was squandered on lavish lifestyles, corrupt contracts, and the purchase of weapons to fuel conflicts.

As the oil flowed out of the country, the promise of prosperity faded into a distant mirage. The people of South Sudan, already impoverished by years of war, were left with nothing but the crushing burden of debt. The government had plundered their future, sacrificing the well-being of generations to come for their short-term gain.

Schools and hospitals crumbled, their walls a testament to the government's disregard for the people. The young, who had once dreamed of a brighter tomorrow, now faced a bleak existence of poverty and despair. The future generations had been betrayed, their hopes and aspirations sold off for a pittance.

The towering mountain of debt grew ever higher, casting a long shadow over the nation. Interest payments consumed the government's budget, leaving no funds for essential services or infrastructure. The people were forced to live in squalor, their dreams crushed beneath the weight of the government's greed.

As the years turned into decades, the legacy of the presold future haunted South Sudan. The nation became a symbol of corruption, mismanagement, and the tragic consequences of mortgaging the future for personal gain. And as the mountain of debt continued to grow, the people of South Sudan were left to ponder the true cost of their government's betrayal.

The Destructive Machine

The air conditioning hummed like a dying insect in the press conference room. The fluorescent lights cast a pale, sterile glow on the faces of the journalists, their eyes trained on the figure seated at the podium. This was no ordinary press conference. This was a spectacle, a performance, a dance of words that, for many, felt more like a dirge.

The spokesperson, a man named Makuac, sat stiffly, his face impassive, his voice a monotone drone. He spoke of peace, of progress, of hope, but his words rang hollow, an echo in the chamber of despair. Each sentence was a carefully crafted bullet, designed to deflect, to deny, to obfuscate. He was a machine, a well-oiled machine of the nation destruction, churning out pronouncements that danced around the truth, ignoring the cries of the people.

Outside the room, the reality was far from the sterile calm of the press conference. The streets were choked with dust, the air thick with the stench of poverty and despair. The hospitals were overflowing, the schools were crumbling, and the fields were barren. The people were hungry, exhausted, and disillusioned. They had heard Makuac's lies before, the promises that never materialized, the hope that was perpetually deferred.

One journalist, a young woman named Nyibol, couldn't bear it anymore. She stood up, her voice trembling with anger. 'How can you speak of peace when there is war in our streets? How can you speak of progress when our children are dying of hunger? How can you speak of hope when our future is being stolen from us?'

Makuac remained impassive. He continued his speech, his voice a relentless drone. He was programmed to ignore, to deflect, to continue the charade. He was a machine, and machines were not designed to feel, to understand, to empathize.

But Nyibol's voice resonated with the other journalists. They began to ask their own questions, their voices rising in a chorus of dissent. They demanded answers, demanded accountability, demanded change. The press conference, once a performance of denial, became a crucible of truth, a space where the voices of the people were finally heard.

The machine, however, remained unmoved. It continued to churn out its pre-programmed responses, its voice a monotonous drone. It was a machine, after all, and machines were not designed to be changed. But the people, the people were different. They were tired of lies, tired of promises that turned to dust. They were tired of being ignored, of being treated like cogs in a machine. They were ready to fight for their future, to reclaim their voice, to demand a better tomorrow. And the machine, the machine of the nation's destruction, would have to face them.

A Prisoner of His Own Conscience

The air conditioning in the conference room hummed, a futile attempt to combat the stifling humidity of Juba. A dozen journalists, faces etched with weary skepticism, sat before the Minister of Finance and Planning, a man named Gabriel who wore a forced smile as wide as the chasm of doubt that separated him from his audience.

'We are injecting millions of dollars into the market,' Gabriel announced, his voice a monotone drone, 'to stimulate the economy and address the ongoing hyperinflation.'

The room remained silent, the only sound the gentle whirring of the air conditioner. Gabriel knew the journalists wouldn't buy it. He knew the truth, the truth that was buried under layers of obfuscation and political pressure.

The truth was, the millions weren't meant to help the people. They were meant to line the pockets of the elite, to prop up the already crumbling facade of a government that had long since lost its legitimacy. Gabriel, a man of integrity once, had been forced to become a puppet, his voice echoing the lies of his superiors.

He remembered the days when he believed in the promise of South Sudan, when he saw hope in the eyes of his fellow countrymen. Now, all he saw was despair, mirrored in the faces of the journalists before him.

'What about the price of food?' a journalist asked, his voice laced with bitterness. 'What about the cost of fuel? How will this money make a difference?'

Gabriel knew the answer. It wouldn't. He knew the money would disappear, swallowed by corruption, leaving the people to fend for themselves. Yet, he was forced to lie.

'We are working tirelessly to address these issues,' he said, his voice flat and devoid of conviction. 'This injection of funds will help to stabilize the economy and bring relief to the people.'

He saw a flicker of doubt in the eyes of the journalists, a flicker that he himself felt deep within his soul. He was a prisoner of his own conscience, forced to betray his principles for the sake of survival.

As the press conference ended, Gabriel walked out, feeling the weight of his hypocrisy crushing him. He knew he couldn't continue this charade. He couldn't be complicit in the destruction of his own country.

But what could he do? He was just one man, a cog in a broken machine, and the forces that controlled him were too powerful.

He walked into the stifling heat of Juba, the air thick with the stench of desperation and despair. He knew he had to do something, but what? The answer, like the future of South Sudan, remained shrouded in uncertainty.

The Architect of Despair

The air hung heavy with the scent of dust and despair. A lone acacia tree stood sentinel in the parched landscape, its branches skeletal against the unforgiving sun. Beneath it, a young woman named Ayen sat, her hands cradling a tattered book. The pages, once vibrant with stories of a brighter future, were now faded and worn, mirroring the hope that had dwindled in her heart.

'Mama, what is this place?' Ayen's son, Deng, a boy of barely five, tugged at her hand, his eyes wide with confusion.

'This is our home, Deng,' she whispered, her voice strained with the weight of unspoken truths. 'But it's a home that has been broken.'

Deng didn't understand. He knew only the harsh reality of their existence – the constant threat of hunger, the fear of violence lurking in the shadows, the absence of a father who had been snatched away by the war. He knew nothing of the promises whispered by the politicians, the peace agreements signed with fanfare, the dreams of a nation that had been born in blood and shattered in betrayal.

Ayen knew all too well. She had witnessed the birth of South Sudan, the jubilant celebrations, the naive hope that had bloomed in the hearts of her people. But the hope had been a fragile flower, easily crushed by the winds of conflict. The promises of peace had turned to dust, the agreements to broken treaties, the dreams to nightmares.

President Salva Kiir, the man who had led them to independence, had become the architect of their despair. His leadership had devolved into a reign of self-preservation, prioritizing power over the well-being of his people. The unity he had promised remained a distant mirage, the tribal divisions festering like open wounds.

'Mama, will we ever have peace?' Deng's question echoed the unspoken longing of every child in South Sudan.

Ayen had no answer. She could only look at her son, his innocent eyes reflecting the pain of a nation, and feel the weight of responsibility crush her. She had been born into war, had witnessed its horrors firsthand, and now, she was forced to witness the same fate befall her son.

Across the country, in the bustling city of Juba, the President sat in his opulent palace, surrounded by advisors and sycophants. The news of the escalating violence in the countryside barely registered. He was preoccupied with solidifying his grip on power, playing a dangerous game of political chess with the lives of his people as pawns.

'The situation is under control, Mr. President,' his chief advisor, a man with a silver tongue and a heart of stone, assured him.

Kiir merely nodded, his gaze distant, his mind preoccupied with the upcoming elections, the power struggles, the ever-present threat of a rival faction seeking to seize control. The plight of his people was a footnote in his grand scheme, a minor inconvenience to be dealt with later.

In a remote village, a young man named Samuel, Deng's father, lay hidden in the bush, his heart heavy with guilt and longing. He had been forced to flee his home, his family separated by the relentless violence. He longed to return, to see his son, to hold his wife, but the fear, the distrust, the shattered trust in his leaders, held him captive.

He had fought for his country, for a future where his son could live in peace. Now, he felt like a traitor, a failed soldier, a man who had lost everything, including the right to hope.

The stories of Ayen, Deng, and Samuel are not unique. They are the echoes of a broken nation, a testament to the failures of its leaders, a chilling reminder that the dreams of independence can be easily extinguished by the flames of greed and ambition. The young generation of South Sudan, born into a war they never asked for, are paying the price of their leaders' betrayal. Their future, once so bright, now hangs precariously in the balance, a fragile hope flickering in the darkness.

A Plan Fueled by Greed

The air in the opulent penthouse was thick with cigar smoke and the scent of expensive perfume. Atop the gleaming marble table, a map of South Sudan lay spread out, its oil fields marked in vibrant red. Around it, five men, their faces etched with the arrogance of power, clinked champagne glasses.

'To hell with the people,' sneered Elias, the youngest of the group, his eyes gleaming with avarice. 'They'll be too busy fighting amongst themselves to notice a few billion dollar missing.'

The others chuckled, nodding in agreement. They were the elite, the architects of the South Sudanese state, and they had a plan. A plan fueled by greed, ambition, and a chilling disregard for the suffering of their own people.

The newly formed nation, fresh from the bloody struggle for independence, was rich in oil. Its black gold, a potential key to prosperity, was also a gateway to unimaginable wealth for those who controlled it. And these men, with their connections and influence, were determined to control it all.

Before the ink had even dried on the peace agreement, they had already secured lucrative agreement contracts with international oil brokers. But their greed knew no bounds. They had also secretly presold the oil, securing billions of dollars in advance, leaving the South

Sudanese government with nothing but empty promises and a crippling debt.

The money flowed into their offshore accounts, fueling lavish lifestyles and hidden investments, while the people of South Sudan were left to grapple with poverty, corruption, and a bloody civil war that tore the country apart.

The whispers started first, murmurs of discontent amongst the people, who began to question the whereabouts of their oil wealth. The government, controlled by the elite, brushed off these concerns, citing the need for development and infrastructure. But the truth was far more sinister.

The elite, their pockets overflowing with ill-gotten gains, were too busy living the high life to care about the plight of their own people. They had sold them out, traded their future for their own insatiable greed.

As the years passed, the consequences of their actions became starkly apparent. The country descended into chaos, its infrastructure crumbling, its people starving, its future bleak. The oil, once a symbol of hope, had become a curse, a reminder of the betrayal of their own leaders.

One day, a young woman named Nyaboth, her eyes burning with anger and a thirst for justice, stood before the men who had betrayed her people. 'You call yourselves leaders?' she spat, her voice trembling with rage. 'You have stolen our future, our wealth, our very lives! But we will not be silenced. We will fight for our country, for our children, for our future!'

Nyaboth's words sparked a fire in the hearts of the people. They rose up, demanding accountability, demanding justice, demanding their rightful share of the oil wealth. The elite, their power crumbling, were left to face the consequences of their actions.

The story of South Sudan, a cautionary tale of greed and betrayal, serves as a stark reminder that true leadership lies not in self-enrichment but in the service of the people. For in the end, it is the people who will determine the fate of their nation, not the elite who seek to exploit them.

A Conquer of Greed

The air hung heavy with the scent of desperation and the acrid tang of betrayal in the dusty office of the Political Parties Council (PPC). A lone, flickering fluorescent bulb cast sickly shadows on the faces of the gathered politicians, each etched with a mixture of anger and resignation. The news had spread like wildfire: the PPC had raised the registration fee for participating in the upcoming elections from a paltry SSP 20,000 to a staggering USD 75,000.

'This is an insult!' thundered a young politician, his voice shaking with indignation. 'They're trying to buy the election outright!'

'It's a blatant attempt to stifle dissent,' echoed another, his face grim. 'They know we can't afford this. They're squeezing us out.'

The room buzzed with murmurs of discontent. The SPLM, once the symbol of hope for a free South Sudan, had devolved into a ruthless machine, using its power to crush any semblance of opposition. The exorbitant fee was just the latest in a series of brazen moves to ensure their stranglehold on power.

A seasoned politician, his face lined with the weariness of countless battles, sighed heavily. 'This is the price of freedom, my friends. We fought for this country, but now it seems the price of participation is beyond the reach of most.'

'But we can't give up!' cried a young woman, her eyes blazing with defiance. 'We have to fight back! We can't let them steal our future!'

The room fell silent, each individual grappling with the weight of the situation. The SPLM's greed had conquered the Political Parties Council, leaving behind a landscape of despair and disillusionment. The dream of a democratic South Sudan, fought for with blood and sacrifice, now seemed to be slipping through their fingers.

But amidst the despair, a flicker of hope remained. The young woman's words resonated, igniting a fire of resistance in the hearts of those present. They knew they were facing an uphill battle, but they refused to surrender.

'We may not have the money,' declared the seasoned politician, his voice now firm with resolve, 'but we have something they underestimate – the will of the people. We will find a way. We will fight. We will not be silenced.'

The room erupted in a chorus of agreement, a defiant roar that echoed through the dusty office, a testament to the indomitable spirit of those who refused to be cowed by the greed of the powerful. The battle for South Sudan's future had just begun, a battle fought not just with money but with the unyielding belief in the power of democracy and the right of the people to choose their own destiny.

A Prisoner of his Own Legacy

The air hung thick with the scent of incense and roasted goat, a stark contrast to the stifling heat of the afternoon sun. Inside the grand tent, draped with vibrantly colored fabrics, Salva Kiir sat upon a throne of carved wood, his face impassive, his eyes reflecting the weight of a nation on his shoulders. Around him, a chorus of voices rose and fell, a symphony of praise for the man they called 'Father of the Nation.'

'Your leadership, Your Excellency, has brought peace and prosperity to our beloved South Sudan!' boomed a voice, emanating from a man with a belly that protruded like a well-fed hippopotamus.

'The oil wells flow like rivers of gold, thanks to your wisdom!' chimed another, a woman with a face painted in intricate designs, her eyes gleaming with an almost fanatical devotion.

Kiir, however, felt a cold knot of dread in his stomach. He knew the reality was far from the rosy picture painted by his sycophants. The oil wells, once a beacon of hope, were now drying up, leaving the nation teetering on the brink of economic ruin. The peace he had promised was a fragile illusion, constantly threatened by simmering tensions between tribes and the incessant rumble of armed factions. The people, once filled with hope for a brighter future, were now burdened by hunger, despair, and the ghosts of a war that never truly ended.

He had come to power with a promise to unite the nation, to build a prosperous future for his people. But the years had turned into a bitter struggle for survival, a constant battle against the demons of corruption, nepotism, and violence that plagued the land. His dreams, once vibrant and hopeful, were now faded and tarnished, a stark reminder of his failures.

As the praise continued, a wave of nausea washed over him. He longed to stand up, to tear down the veil of lies and expose the truth, to scream at the top of his lungs that he had failed them, that he was not the savior they believed him to be.

But he remained seated, his face a mask of stoicism, his silence a testament to the powerlessness he felt. He knew that speaking the truth would only bring him more enemies, more threats, more instability. So he sat, enduring the nauseating barrage of praise, a prisoner of his own legacy, a king in a crumbling kingdom.

As the sun dipped below the horizon, casting long shadows across the tent, Kiir stood, the weight of the nation pressing down on his shoulders. He knew that the truth, like a festering wound, would eventually seep through the cracks of the facade, leaving behind a nation scarred and broken. But for now, he could only offer a hollow smile and a silent prayer for a future he could no longer see.

A Conduit for Personal Fortune

The sun beat down on the dusty road, a cruel reminder of the sweltering heat that clung to Juba like a shroud. A battered Land Cruiser, its paint job faded to a sickly yellow, rumbled past, kicking up a cloud of dust that settled on the parched earth. Inside, Elias, a man whose belly had grown with the country's wealth, chuckled. He was on his way to inspect the new road, a project he'd spearheaded, or rather, 'overseen' – a euphemism for the blatant self-enrichment that had become the norm in South Sudan.

The road, a ribbon of asphalt stretching towards the horizon, was a monument to Elias's cunning. He had used his connection in the presidency to secure a hefty contract, claiming it was vital for national development.

In reality, the project was a conduit for his personal fortune. The crude oil, the lifeblood of the nation, flowed through his veins, not the veins of the country. He'd siphoned off funds, inflated prices, and skimmed profits, leaving behind a road that was more pothole than pavement.

The project had been touted as a symbol of progress, a testament to South Sudan's newfound independence. On paper, it was a marvel of engineering, a shining example of how the country's oil wealth was being used to build a better future. In reality, it was a testament to Elias's greed, a monument to the corruption that was eating away at the nation's soul.

Elias stopped the Land Cruiser, stepping out into the oppressive heat. He surveyed the road, a smirk playing on his lips. The potholes were a testament to his ingenuity – a clever way of padding his pockets. He had deliberately used inferior materials, knowing that the road would deteriorate quickly, requiring constant repairs, and thus, more money for him.

He glanced at the workers, their faces etched with weariness and despair. They were paid a pittance, their lives a daily struggle for survival. Elias felt no guilt, no pang of conscience. They were just pawns in his game, expendable tools in his quest for wealth.

As he drove back towards Juba, the setting sun casting long shadows across the dusty landscape, Elias couldn't help but feel a sense of satisfaction. He had played the game, and he had won. The road, a symbol of progress, was a reminder of his victory. But it was also a symbol of the country's downfall, a testament to the insidious corruption that was slowly killing South Sudan.

The oil, the nation's hope, was being bled dry, not for the benefit of the people, but for the enrichment of a few. And as the sun dipped below the horizon, casting the land in an ominous red glow, Elias knew that he had played his part in this slow, agonizing death. He had traded the future of his country for his own selfish desires, and he knew that the consequences would be far-reaching and devastating. But he was too far gone, too consumed by his own greed to care. The road, a symbol of his victory, was also a symbol of South Sudan's demise, a testament to the power of corruption to destroy even the most hopeful of nations.

The Promise of Wealth

The sun beat down on the dusty road, baking the cracked asphalt and turning the air into a shimmering mirage. Atop a rickety truck, Elias, a young man with eyes as deep and dark as the oil-rich earth beneath him, watched the landscape blur by. He was on his way to Juba, the capital of South Sudan, carrying a file that held the promise of wealth – not for his people, but for himself.

Elias wasn't born into privilege. His life had been a constant struggle, a relentless dance with poverty and hunger. He had seen his family struggle to survive, their dreams choked by the relentless grip of hardship. This oil, this black gold, held the key to a different life, a life free from the chains of poverty. It was a life he was willing to claw his way into, even if it meant turning his back on his own people.

The journey to Juba was long and arduous, the road riddled with potholes and choked by dust. Elias, however, was focused on the prize – the lucrative contracts he had secured for himself, contracts that would make him a billionaire. He had used his connections, his charm, and his ruthlessness to secure these deals, playing the corrupt system to his advantage. He knew the rules of the game, the unwritten laws of greed that governed this land.

In Juba, the city pulsed with a feverish energy, fueled by the oil boom. Individuals' buildings rose like steel and glass monoliths, their shadows stretching long and menacing across the dusty streets. Elias felt a thrill of excitement, a sense of belonging amidst this chaotic prosperity. He had arrived, he had made it.

He met with his clients, men whose faces were etched with the same ruthless ambition that burned within him. They spoke in hushed tones, their words laced with cynicism and greed. Elias played his part, his voice smooth and persuasive, his promises grand. The deals were struck, the money exchanged, and Elias was on his way to becoming a man of wealth and influence.

But as the days turned into weeks, and the weeks into months, a gnawing unease began to settle in Elias's gut.

He saw the stark contrast between the opulent lifestyles of the elite and the abject poverty of the majority. He saw the infrastructure crumbling, the roads pockmarked, the schools and hospitals underfunded. The oil wealth, the very thing that had brought him prosperity, was fueling a system that was systematically robbing his people of their future.

His conscience, long dormant, began to stir. He saw the children, their eyes hollow with hunger, their bodies frail and emaciated. He saw the mothers, their faces etched with despair, their dreams shattered by the cruel hand of fate. He saw the fathers, their spirits broken, their hope extinguished by the relentless cycle of poverty.

Elias started to question his choices, his actions. The guilt, like a heavy stone, began to weigh him down. He realized that the wealth he had amassed came at a terrible price, a price paid by his own people, a price that was slowly eroding their very humanity.

One day, he saw a group of children playing in the dusty streets, their laughter echoing through the air. He watched them, their innocent joy a stark contrast to the despair that surrounded them. A wave of compassion washed over him, a wave that threatened to drown him in its intensity.

He knew he had to do something, had to make things right. The guilt had become unbearable, the weight of his conscience too heavy to bear. He had to break free from the cycle of greed, from the system that had enslaved him and his people.

He reached out to a group of activists, men and women who had dedicated their lives to fighting for the rights of the marginalized. He shared his story, his guilt, his newfound desire to change. They listened, their faces etched with a mixture of skepticism and hope.

Elias knew the road ahead would be long and arduous, filled with challenges and setbacks. But he was determined, driven by a newfound sense of purpose, a desire to make amends for the wrongs he had committed. He knew he couldn't undo the past, but he could fight for a better future, a future where the wealth of the land would be shared by all, where the oil that had brought him riches would become the foundation for a brighter tomorrow. The journey to redemption, he knew, had just begun.

Made in the USA
Middletown, DE
22 June 2024

55875965R00136